BERLIN

LUKE RICHARDSON

1

Keal knew there was nothing like the kiss of a pistol in the night. The cold pressure of the exterminating snout against your forehead. He recognised it instantly, even before opening his eyes.

What joker is this? He thought. Probably some hoodlums from Marzhan who've seen the Porsche outside and decided to try their luck. *Fair enough.* Keal smiled to himself. It was a nice car. Let them try. They wouldn't get far once they realised who he was.

With his eyes closed, Keal listened to the room around him. How many of these *ukolovs* were there? More than one, surely.

Footsteps shuffled and squeaked across the wooden floor by the door. So, there must be two men at least. That was sensible of them. If this *pridurok* was alone, then holding the gun to Keal's face would be his last act on this earth.

Keal heard the fridge click and begin to rumble. They must have left the door through to the kitchen open. The thudding engine of a motorbike passed in the street and then faded back into the city. It sounded distant, which meant the apartment door was shut. That was the right thing for them to do; they wouldn't want a show like this to get interrupted before the interval. Ten out of ten so far.

Keal could tell quite a lot about a man by the way he held his gun. Inexperienced wide-boys tended to jab the weapon at their opponents as though it was some kind of bayonet. As though the tip itself was going to cause them damage. Keal knew that wasn't the way to do it. A gun in a play for power was like a delicate spice. You used it carefully to bring the dish alive. This guy, Keal realised, knew that too. The cold ring of the snout was pressed lightly against his head. Just enough to let him know it was there. Not enough to put pressure on the holder's forearm. The hand was steady and firm too. That was good, for his opponent at least.

And if Keal wasn't mistaken — he concentrated now — the business end of the gun was thicker than usual. This man was using a silencer. The Cold War had finished a long time ago. Nowadays, gunshots drew attention. Keal knew this more than most.

Keal exhaled slowly. They were doing well but had made one fatal error. Their choice of target. Did they not know who Keal was? Were they that *yeblya* stupid they thought they could rob one of Olezka Ivankov's men and get away with it?

Just a small-time crook as the wall fell, Olezka used the country's reunification to set himself up. While others were celebrating their newfound unity, Olezka was establishing trade lines with the Russian Bratva, South American Cartels and organised criminals all across Europe. It was fair to say, now thirty years on, very little criminal activity happened in Berlin that he didn't know something about. And the *Vor v*

Zakone — the kingpin — was ruthless. Anyone who got in his way was found floating in the Spree. Keal had dumped more bodies than he could count beneath its murky water over the last fifteen years. He and Olezka were close. These little idiots could have their fun now, but it wouldn't last long.

The woman beside Keal exhaled and rolled over, dragging her hand from where it had rested on his stomach. Her dark hair fanned out on the pillow behind her. Keal quelled a fleeting shard of worry — she didn't matter. He wasn't sure he could remember her name anyway.

It had been a fun night. Women enjoyed a man with a lot of money and recreational drugs — and Keal enjoyed the women. Sure, he'd paid this one, but that was all part of the fun.

He thought about the bottle of whiskey on the bedside table. He would have a swig as soon as he'd dealt with these idiots.

Right, Keal thought, preparing to open his eyes. *Let's see what these priduroks have got to say.*

"After all these years you thought you could rob from me?" came the voice, as though answering his thoughts. Keal's breath caught in his throat, and his eyes shot open. The room was gloomy. Shards of orange light streamed through the blind and cast horizontal bars on the floor. By this light, Keal's worst suspicions were confirmed.

"Olezka," Keal said, his mouth suddenly dry. "What are you —"

"Shut up," Olezka replied, his voice gravelly. "Get up. We're going for a drive."

2

"The night is always darker in the East."

The usual cigarette-fuelled Russian accent was closer than he expected. Its warmth grazed his cheek.

"But you've never seen rain like we get in the West."

He gave the planned reply. The expected reply. It sounded futile against the techno beat from the nightclub's dancefloor. The thud rattled and groaned through the thick curtain that kept the light at bay. In a way, it was all futile. He knew that. But this was his last chance. His last and only chance.

He could smell the other man in the darkness. He was sure of it. The thick, pungent scent of tobacco and the sweet tang of vodka. Had his sense of smell become more defined after just a few minutes in complete darkness? Or was his imagination in overdrive?

The owner of the voice didn't respond. Light streamed in as the curtain was pulled aside.

He squinted. The nightclub's bright lights stung.

"Okay, follow me."

Berlin

Stepping out into the nightclub, he looked around. Lights around the dancefloor strobed and flickered. Large parts of the space lay in enigmatic darkness. The chaos of the rave. It was all so alien now. Pulsing bodies prickled with sweat. The upstretched hands. Puckered lips and shimmering sunglasses. He'd been there before, getting lost in the music. The never-ending beat. Now he just wanted out.

He looked back at the space behind the curtain — the darkroom. Before coming to Berlin, he'd never seen anything like it. Just a dark corner of the dancefloor covered by a thick curtain to keep light and prying eyes away. What happened in there was no one's business.

As he watched, two women stepped past him into the darkness. The eyes of a tattooed eagle stared malevolently from the shoulder of one. The woman looked from him to the Russian and back again. A wry smile curled her lips. Worry fluttered through him. She couldn't think he was —

It didn't matter now. Not anymore.

He glanced ahead and saw the Russian merge into the swaying crowd. He dropped the curtain on the two women, already in each other's arms, and rushed to keep up.

He and the Russian had met several times. The Russian was one of the men who came to the shop to collect the packages. In his imagination, he invented names and identities for these silent patrons — the men whose piles of dirty money had kept his business afloat for many years. The man with the long green coat and eyes the colour of Berlin's winter sky was one of his favourites. Unlike most of the men, he wasn't just a thug. There was intelligence in the stare. He had to trust that stare tonight. Tonight, it was getting personal. Tonight, was his only chance to escape. But for it all to work, everything needed to be just right.

As instructed, he'd arrived at the club just after

midnight. He'd nursed a succession of beers as the hours crawled past. As the techno beat clattered across the baying crowd, he'd counted the minutes until they met behind the curtain at four.

Why did they have to meet here, anyway? The secret meeting place and coded introductions were all a bit over the top. The Cold War was supposed to have finished a long time ago. Maybe old habits really did die hard.

Beyond the dancefloor up ahead the Russian turned left into a passage. They couldn't get separated now. He shouted apologies as he pressed between a pair of dancing women. They smiled back — no problems here.

The Russian strode on, coat billowing.

Two different techno beats echoed fitfully from damp bricks walls. To the left, the strobes fired above the heads of black-clad dancers.

The nightclub was a fitting place to end it. The reason he came to Berlin in the first place. It was almost poetic. Poetry that, for some reason, he thought the slender Russian striding ahead would understand. It was as though he'd chosen the place on purpose.

They turned into the main bar area. Smoke and anticipation hung thick in the air as people queued for drinks — bottles of water, vodka and beer.

Following the Russian was becoming easier. People moved aside as he approached. It wasn't that he looked tough; there was just something about him, something in those grey-blue eyes that exuded a warning.

The Russian shoved through a fire escape. He followed.

The air outside felt crisp and refreshing. Each breath, nourishing. Each inhalation brought hope. People continued to queue around the nightclub's main entrance.

Berlin

For Berlin, the night was young. The sky above was clear. Spears of crimson warned of dawn's imminent arrival.

For him, it was at an end. It was all at an end.

3

Leo lies back and looks up at the tropical sky. Twilight ribbons of pink and purple drain in pursuit of the sinking sun. The night is coming, and there's nowhere he'd rather be right now. He knows that with more certainty than ever.

The noise of the jungle swells in the silence. A bird calls and another answers. Two animals yammer to one another. Sea and sand tumble together. The sounds of paradise.

Next to him on the jetty sits a woman. Her feet dangle in the lapping waves.

"How did we get here? I mean, this is crazy — it's like a different world," Leo says, unable to take his eyes from the darkening sky. They've been travelling around Asia for the last two months. First India, then Vietnam. Now Thailand. They're on the island of Koh Tao for the final few nights. They're clinging to the feeling of freedom before the flight home beckons.

For a moment he thinks about his job; he works as a journalist for a local paper. That's if the editor will even have him back — he was supposed to have returned a month ago.

But it doesn't seem important right now; their ordinary lives are a million miles away.

"Koh Tao is a special place because it's hard to get to," she says without looking at him. "When things are hard to find, that's when they're precious."

She's right. Leo knows it. He's spent years looking for her, years looking for someone who makes him feel complete. Someone who makes him feel normal, let alone happy. He sits up on his elbows and looks at her. Her feet dangle in the water, and her smile is currency across the world.

With an uncharacteristic certainty, he knows this is the moment he's been waiting for. This is perfect.

"I'm just glad to be here... with you," he says. Then, with quickening breath, he fumbles with his wallet. That's where the ring's been hidden for over a month. That's how long he's been waiting for this moment. Waiting to ask this question. "I'm so glad to be here, even the extra month..."

Every day he's thought about this. Waiting for the perfect moment.

It has to be right. It has to be perfect.

This time. This moment. This woman.

He pulls the ring from the wallet and places it on the palm of his hand. Then he sits up and looks back at her. She is beautiful. He's always known that. Darkened by the sun, her complexion looks more akin to that of her Kenyan mother — Leo imagines that, anyway. She's tied her hair in a bright headscarf. Thickly curled strands fall from each side.

Leo pulls a deep breath and steadies his nerves. The air tastes of salt, tamarind and lime. To Leo, it smells of hope, opportunity and love.

He holds the breath for a moment. He feels the exhilaration. Then he lets it go.

"Will you —" he begins.

"We're here," a voice interrupts.

Leo ignores it, stuttering over his words.

"Will you..."

"Leo, wake up, we're here!"

An eddy of cold wind rushes in. Leo shivers.

"Oi! Wake up!"

4

Keal watched the darkened streets of Berlin pass in a blur beyond the car window. He had dressed hurriedly with the dead eye of Olezka's pistol never leaving him, and was led out of the apartment and into the King Pin's Rolls Royce. In the movies, these things always looked dramatic. People were bundled, fighting all the way from one place to the next. In reality, Keal knew that didn't happen. If someone didn't do what you required, then a bullet was promptly lodged between their eyes and they were driven down to the river. No arguments. *Only five minutes ago,* Keal thought as he glanced at the softly glowing clock on the dash, *I was asleep.*

"What is this about?" Keal forced a laugh into his voice. "Is this some kind of joke?"

The unblinking pistol stared at him in the deadly silence. Keal clenched and opened his hands three times. He glanced up at the boss. Despite Olezka's age, he was in good shape. His tall body looked as though it was carved in marble straight from the mines of Kolegamarmor. Even with half the miles on the clock, Keal didn't think he could take the man hand for hand.

"Am I supposed to have done something? I can assure you, whatever it is, I haven't done it."

The Mafia boss watched silently as the city streamed past. The buildings became increasingly sparse the further they got from the city.

"Look at that," Olezka said as he pointed through the window. A row of decrepit warehouses lined the road beyond which the sky was beginning to lighten.

"What, the buildings?"

"No, not the buildings you idiot, the sky."

Keal looked at the reddening sky announcing the coming dawn.

"Yes sir, it's getting light."

"You know there was a phrase I once heard," Olezka said as he looked at Keal. "Red sky in the morning is a warning. Or something like that." His flicked his free hand.

Keal didn't reply.

"It means that we have to be careful today because something bad might happen. You know what I mean?"

"Yes boss," Keal replied. A growing wave of nausea surged through him.

The car slowed and turned from the main road. They passed between two monolithic factories, their walls dark against the lightening sky, their chimneys smokeless.

The road became unpaved, and the car began to bounce. They crawled forward as gravel skittered beneath the tyres.

Turning again, they pulled into a yard and the car crunched to a stop

"We're here," Olezka said, waiting for his driver to come and open the door.

Berlin

Keal looked out at the building. He thought he knew all of the locations they used. This one was new.

Two strong torches snapped on and swung towards the car. They dazzled Keal as they neared. Keal noticed the men carrying the torches also had automatic rifles. Keal recognised the men, a pair of junior jokers called Semion and Konstantin. Keal's good humour didn't extend to these arseholes. They were part of a new generation making their way through the ranks of the organisation. Having learned to fire a gun on a computer game, they now thought they knew it all. As far as Keal was concerned, they were nothing but pond life.

Konstantin opened the door while Semion dazzled Keal with the torch's strong beam.

"Take him in and get him ready," Olezka said.

Keal stood obediently and straightened up. He was four inches taller than Konstantin. Konstantin snarled and attempted to seize Keal's arm. Keal was quicker than that. He flicked his hand upwards and slapped Konstantin in the face.

Konstantin's face flushed red as he levelled the gun at Keal.

"I can walk on my own, you *blyad*. Touch me again, and I'll snap your hand off," Keal snarled.

"Just get him in there," Olezka barked from behind them.

Keal walked towards the building. With each step he thought about the two automatic rifles aimed at his back.

5
———

Out on the street, he dropped behind the Russian. He had to look as though he was leaving the club alone. The CCTV footage may be checked. The problem was, he didn't know where they were going. It all depended on schedules and shift patterns, apparently. But it *was* going to happen tonight.

The nightclub's techno thud became distant as they turned a corner — the heat, the sweat and the fluid movement of the dancers were now just a hazy memory.

Cars passed dozily on the street. It was still before dawn. That strange time when people waking for work mingled with those not yet asleep. The present and future coexisting for a few nebulous minutes.

A taxi slowed in search of a fare. Keeping his eyes on the Russian, he waved it off.

Ahead, the road straightened alongside a railway. Confident he could see the man from a distance on the straight road, he dropped his pace. For ten minutes, they walked through a patchwork of glaring streetlight and hanging shadows.

Tattered posters advertising events he would never attend flapped in the breeze.

He reached Warschauer Strasse S-Bahn station and followed the Russian inside. They waited at opposite ends of the empty platform. People could still be watching.

The sky continued to lighten. Spikes of bruised purple scudded across the blue. Soon the whole city would be awake. Another Berlin day. A day like any other.

His eyes were drawn to a pair of small birds skipping through the sky. They darted this way and that. Their twittering song sounded sharp and shrill in the still morning air.

The city, the world, the morning — all were coming alive. A motorbike grunted beyond the walls of the station. A group of people climbed the stairs and their voices echoed across the platform. Two birds came to rest on a wire and considered him with their dark eyes. Maybe they were leaving the city soon too, heading south perhaps. Bouncing from the wire, they pounded into the still air. It would be a duller city without them.

The rails began to snap and ring. A train was coming.

Alles aussteigen bitte, Endstation – all change.

The doors of the bright yellow train hissed open, and a dozen sleepy passengers tumbled out. The Russian got on, and he followed. They stood at opposite ends of the same car. Waiting for departure, he found himself examining the dark wooden veneer of the train's interior, embellished by the scrawls of many years. He wanted to drink in the details. Save them for some future time. Trains like this were a piece of the city. They were as important as the Brandenburg Gate or the Love Parade. They were a part of the place, the very fabric of it, just like he had been.

As the train pulled from the station, a realisation struck

him. This city had been his home for the last five years. But after tonight it was all over. He may never see the city again. It was sad, but there was no other way. He had to get out. He had to go.

He watched the shimmering water through the window as they crossed the river. The lights of some modern boxy office buildings built on the sites of East German warehouses glowed ethereally. Above it all, the spire of the *Berliner Fernsehturm* — the Television Tower — clawed the sky.

For a few seconds, the view seemed unchanged, and then they were swallowed by the chaotic rooftops of Kreuzberg. This was his neighbourhood. These vibrant, diverse and energetic streets had been his kingdom.

This was what he wanted — what he needed. There was no other way.

As the train slowed for Kottbusser Tor, the Russian began to move. The four stops felt like ten. Keeping his distance and without looking directly at the Russian, he followed. Things needed to look normal. There could be no suspicions.

Above, the day was anxious to break. The sky's dome, washed with blue, pleaded for him to stay. He looked greedily at the nimbus shapes flushed with shades of fuchsia and mauve. He drank it in through the dirty windows in the station's iron canopy. He pulled his last breath of the Berlin dawn. The final inhalation of a suffocating man.

Then, he followed the Russian underground.

6

"Oi! Wake up!"

Leo forced his eyes open. It felt as though each one contained a handful of sand — a physical manifestation of his dream, perhaps.

He blinked hard and shook his head. The light stung.

"We're here," Allissa said from her seat across the aisle. "You slept through the entire landing. We all had to hear your snoring."

Leo rubbed his face. "What? We're what..."

"We have just landed at London Gatwick Airport." Allissa mimicked the pilot's plummy voice. "And the local time is —"

"Alright, alright. I get it."

"And the outside temperature is... bloody freezing. And I think it's raining."

People scrambled to their feet around them. They stood, bent double, beneath the overhead luggage compartments.

Leo sighed and pushed his shoulder blades together. The man next to him stood and attempted to retrieve his bag from the compartment above.

"They've not even opened the doors yet," Leo groaned. "No point getting up."

Leo blinked again, trying to remove the colours that danced across his vision. This was typical. He'd sat awake for the first seven and a half hours of the flight, twisting and turning with every movement and sound. Then he'd fallen asleep just before landing.

At least it wasn't as bad as their flight from Hong Kong to Abu Dhabi, Leo thought. On that flight, three days before, he'd finally managed to get to sleep just as the person beside him needed the toilet. Instead of shaking Leo awake with an apology, the man had attempted to climb over him. Although Leo knew this came from a place of courtesy, it didn't mitigate the confusion of waking to find yourself straddled by a stranger.

Finally, as people began to shuffle forward, Leo pushed out of his seat. It wasn't fair. Allissa just seemed to close her eyes during the safety video and sleep the whole way. Why couldn't he? At least now they were going home to rest.

Weaving through the crowds in the direction of the train station, Leo realised he didn't even know what time it was. Beside him, Allissa — bright-eyed and rejuvenated — led them towards the correct platform.

Although the case in Hong Kong had been trying for them both, Leo had found it emotionally draining. More through luck than design, he'd finally caught up with the woman who'd forced him into the world of missing people. All told he'd spent over two years looking for her. Countless days. Innumerable hours. Throughout that time, though, he'd never considered what he would actually do if he found her. Talk to her, he supposed, try to understand why she left. In reality, however, he had no idea what to say or do. It was like looking at an oil-covered beach or a desiccated forest. They had once been something beautiful and pure. But not anymore.

For the last three days, Leo and Allissa had been staying in a five-star hotel in Abu Dhabi. Since they had to stop there anyway, Allissa suggested they make the most of it. They'd spent the time in their twin beds watching American comedies on the giant TV, visited the resort's spa and pools, and eaten in the lavish restaurants. Allissa had found it therapeutic, but to Leo, it had been the opposite.

Lying sleepless on that first night, he knew why. Before finding Mya, he and Allissa's relationship was simple. They got on and enjoyed spending time together. And they were pretty damn good at finding missing people. Meaning that, whether Leo liked it or not, he and Allissa had landed themselves with a bonafide business.

It was a business that required them both, though, Leo knew that. Although they were both resourceful investigators, Allissa was the driving force behind the business. Money, to Leo — providing his credit cards still worked — was an irrelevance. To Allissa, it was a way of life. She seemed to understand what they needed for each job. She discussed sums with clients that made Leo squirm. She made the bookings, then allocated funds and somehow ensured there was enough left over for them to make a profit.

She also had a fierce sense of right and wrong. Where Leo might have been ready to give up on an investigation, Allissa would carry on until all the ends were tied. But it wasn't her business acumen or her investigatory prowess that now worried Leo.

Before Leo had caught up with Mya, things between Allissa and himself were simple. He was looking for Mya. But now that door was closed, Leo could do what he wanted.

That brought with it a wave of mayhem, misunderstanding and misery. There was no longer anything in the way.

Watching Allissa's eyes flick across the landscape, Leo knew that things had changed. A different feeling was smouldering now, and Leo didn't think he liked it.

7

"Just tell me what this is about?" Keal groaned.

There was no point trying to run. The two men behind him carried weapons capable of firing ten bullets a second. And even if he did by some miracle make it away from them, Olezka's reach through the underground networks was long. There weren't many places you could go that the *Vor v Zakone* didn't have a contact. But it was all just some big misunderstanding. He would just have to wait and find out what it was.

What worried Keal though, was that Olezka was never that bothered about finding out the truth. Although Olezka was the judge and jury, he usually jumped straight to his role as executioner before asking any questions.

In the torches' twin beams, Keal saw something scurry away from them down the dilapidated corridor. Whatever it was, it had a fleshy tail as thick as a thumb.

"Turn right," Semion said.

Keal obliged, and the men followed. Two fingers of light from the torches swept through the room. As far as Keal could see, the place was abandoned. Bare concrete walls bore the scars of decay and graffiti. Some of the windows were bricked up, and others had no glass. The bough of a tree extended through one.

Keal heard the faint whine and thud of a petrol generator and then the room filled with light.

The room was large with thick concrete pillars. It sat empty except for a metal chair in the centre. Seeing the chair, Keal felt his knuckles clench. This really wasn't looking good.

"Sit down," came a voice from behind him.

"What, I really haven't —"

Keal didn't finish his sentence as he was struck from behind with the barrel of a gun. The room shuddered. Keal did everything he could to stay on his feet.

"Look you *kolot,* you're done for." Keal heard Konstatin whispering behind him. "I would put a bullet in you now, but Olezka wants a word. So just do what you're told."

Keal's anger welled as Konstantin jabbed the muzzle of the rifle in his back.

Such an amateur. Who did this little prick think he was? Keal wasn't going to be treated like that.

"Move now," Konstantin said. Keal felt the man's breath on the back of his neck.

Big mistake.

Swiping his hand behind him, Keal pushed the barrel of the gun to the side. The man squeezed the trigger. Two shots zipped harmlessly into the concrete. Spinning on the ball of his right foot, Keal forced his knee into the other man's kidney and pushed the gun upwards. The barrel of the rifle now nestled against Konstantin's chin. Konstantin's thick lips quivered as Keal leaned over the smaller man.

"Don't fuck with me," Keal hissed. Spittle flew from his mouth. Keal closed his hand around the man's trigger finger and began to squeeze. "You don't fancy shooting yourself, do you?"

All expression slipped from Konstantin's face as he realised Keal was serious. His mouth began to move like a fish out of water.

Keal forced Konstantin's hand from the trigger and took the position himself.

"Turn around," Keal whispered.

Konstantin turned, and Keal gripped him hard around the neck with his left arm while holding the gun with his right. This felt natural to Keal. This was what he did.

The whole exchange had taken less than two seconds.

"Somebody," Keal shouted, "needs to tell me what the fuck is going on here!"

Semion, who had turned for just a few seconds to switch on the generator, looked back in shock. His fingers groped for the trigger as he raised the gun towards Keal.

"Well?" Keal said. "You wake me up and drag me to this shit hole, for what?"

Semion raised the gun even higher and took aim. Keal could see his hand shaking.

This guy is so green.

Keal's eyes narrowed. This was some hangover.

"Keal, what are you going to do?" Olezka's deep burr came from the door. "Shoot him?"

Olezka stepped into the room, his thick-set body and shaven head silhouetted against the bright light. In his right hand, the silenced pistol pointed squarely at Keal.

"Now what exactly would shooting this man achieve? You would still be here. We would still have the conversation we are going to have. Except he would be dead."

Pulling a deep breath, Keal ran through his options. He didn't want to piss off Olezka. For one, he liked the man.

Secondly, pissing off Olezka was pretty much a death sentence.

"Dedushka Olezka, I don't want to piss you off. But I can't have *lokhi* like this pushing me around."

"I see," Oleka said, nodding his head. His sweat-dappled scalp glimmered beneath the lights.

"I respect you Dedushka Olezka, I'm just not sure —"

Keal was interrupted by a whisper from Olezka's silenced pistol. His thick hand merely swayed with the recoil. Keal felt a shudder as the bullet passed neatly through Konstantin's head. The man went limp and slid to the floor.

Keal's jaw dropped. Blood and brains coated the front of his clothes. The bullet had burrowed through the man's head and missed Keal by less than an inch.

"Problem solved," Olezka said. "We can't have him pushing you around, can we?" The pistol was now levelled directly between Keal's eyes. Olezka's face contorted into a grin. Without even being asked, Keal felt himself slide the rifle to the floor.

"That's good," Olezka said. "We're just going to have a conversation. Is that okay with you?"

Keal nodded.

"Semion, tie his hands," Olezka said. "We can't have any more accidents. And find out where Borya is, he needs to be here. Oh, and take Konstantin outside. We'll dump him in the Spree later."

8

"Are you looking forward to seeing Archie and Lucy?" Leo asked as the taxi sped through the streets of Brighton towards their flat. Large coffees imbibed on the train had seemed to help. Now Leo could see straight and almost hold a normal conversation.

"Yes," Allissa said, "though I'm not sure what it'll be like. We've not really spoken for years."

Archie and Lucy were Allissa's older half brother and sister. After learning what their father had done to her mother, Allissa had cut all contact with the family. Seeing them again, after her father was finally sent to prison, they had all promised to keep in touch. At the time, Allissa had doubted it. So, when she'd received an invitation to Lucy's birthday party, Allissa knew she had to attend.

"Are you sure you'll be alright without me for a day? What're you going to do on your own?"

"Can't wait," Leo said, not turning from the window. Through the glass, the grey city streamed past. It already felt as though it was closing in around him. The flat they were returning to had been cold and empty for weeks. There would be washing to do and mail to sort — the general business of society from which Leo took no joy.

"It'll be good to have a chance to tidy the place up," Leo said.

"You sure? You can come if you want?"

"No, thanks." Leo turned to face Allissa. "I'm going to get some sleep and try to catch up on the invoices we've not done for ages. Then we can afford to eat next week."

Allissa tried to suppress a grin. She doubted Leo even knew how to raise an invoice.

The taxi rounded a corner, and the sea flickered into view between the buildings. It looked grey and sombre, a world away from the azure blue of the pool they'd been in the day before.

"Just on the right here," Allissa said as the taxi turned into their street. The large Victorian houses lining the street looked drab and bleak in the grey morning. "Thanks, just —" Allissa shouted as the taxi driver shot past their house. Registering what Allissa had said over his phone conversation, the driver slammed to a stop and began to reverse.

"Honestly." Leo sighed. "It's fine, just here will do."

The taxi driver punched a button on the metre and pointed to the price.

Leo eased out his wallet and looked inside.

"Got any cash?" Leo asked.

Allissa shook her head.

"Can I use my card?"

The taxi driver scowled. He apparently disliked the idea of Leo's payment going through the traditional channels as much as he disliked the idea of stopping in the right place. When Leo laid out the alternative of receiving his fare in Hong Kong Dollars, the taxi driver conceded that the card payment was better than that "funny money".

The car sped off the moment Leo and Allissa were clear of the vehicle.

Above them, a pair of seagulls flashed from one building to another. Hearing their sorrowful shrieking, Leo looked up. That was a real Brighton sound. Now he knew he was back.

9

He descended the stairs and heard the whine and hiss of a train accelerating away. For him, that was the sound of Berlin. A sound unlike any other metro train in the world. For five years, a sound that had made this place feel like home.

He glanced around the quiet platform. Every sound and sight was valuable this morning. A group of young people returning from a night out slumped onto a bench. A man with dreadlocks nodded to music on large headphones. Somewhere far off another train rumbled like a nightmare in another sleeper's head.

The Russian reached the end of the platform and stopped.

The place needed to be exact.

Laughter from the young people rolled like thunder.

The Russian checked his watch.

That's the sign.

He pulled out his phone and selected his brother's number. It was the only number saved on the unfamiliar handset. With a wave of guilt, he placed the phone to his ear.

Was he really doing this? There was no other way. If there was, he'd have taken it. He needed to get out.

The call connected to the answering service, as he knew it would. It wasn't yet 4 am in Brighton. There wouldn't be enough time to say everything with less than a minute. The words came slowly.

A roar from the tunnel prophesied the coming train. This was it.

Glancing at the Russian, he stepped forwards.

The train burst into the station. A flurry of warm air and purring motors. It wouldn't stop yet.

Stepping forward, he teetered on the edge — the precipice.

The approaching rumble vibrated through the soles of his feet. Shook his knees. Hips. Spine. He closed his eyes tightly and felt the oncoming train in his veins.

The brakes whined and hissed. It was slowing. But it would be too late.

10

"Oh great, my dress has arrived," Allissa said, stepping into their flat's communal entrance hall. Before being split into apartments, the top one of which was Leo and Allissa's, the house would have been grand. The entrance hall hinted at this with its intricate plaster mouldings and patterned floor tiles.

"I ordered it while we were in Abu Dhabi," Allissa said, holding up the package.

"Did you, I don't remember? I hope it fits," Leo said, following Allissa up to their flat.

Leo dropped the suitcases in the middle of the front room and looked around. The place was a mess, just as he remembered. The discoloured paint had begun to peel from the walls, and the carpet was threadbare. His computer sat on a desk in the bay window amid piles of books and papers.

There had been discussions about them moving somewhere better now that the business was doing alright. But, with the amount of time they'd been away, neither had done anything about it.

"Yeah, glad it's here," Allissa said. She filled the kettle and clicked it on. "I'm going to have a quick shower and try it on." Allissa held up the package. "Tell me what you think."

"Sure," Leo said. "I need another coffee first, though. Want one?"

"Yes, please," Allissa said, heading in the direction of her bedroom.

Before Allissa moved in, her bedroom had been unused. The rent in the rundown apartment was so cheap that Leo had never even considered having a housemate. But he had to admit; he liked having Allissa there.

Leo walked into the kitchen as the kettle grumbled to the boil. He grabbed the canister of instant coffee, pulled off the lid and began to spoon it into a cup. Then, with a smile, he remembered Allissa had pranked him two weeks ago by swapping the canisters around. Leo suppressed a giggle and pulled the 'Tea' canister from the shelf. There was no way he was going to acknowledge the change and let Allissa win.

"Coffee's on the table," Leo said as Allissa entered the front room. He was lying back on the sofa with his eyes shut. "There's no milk, I'm afraid. Or rather, there is milk, but it's been there for so long it's developed its own ecosystem. To be fair, you take your life in your hands even by opening the fridge —"

"What do you think?" Allissa said, interrupting him.

"Well, it's pretty gross, we should have emptied it before we left —"

"No, what do you think about the dress?"

Leo opened his eyes and sat up. His eyes widened, and his jaw dropped.

Having known each other for almost a year, and lived together for a few months, Leo and Allissa had seen each other in many different states. Leo was used to looking away as Allissa passed him wrapped in a towel or only wearing her underwear. Those things, however, did nothing to prepare him for what he saw now.

As his eyes ran across her body, Leo felt himself smile. The black dress glimmered across the swell of her chest and clung to the pinch of her waist.

"What's... You don't like it?" Alissa asked, turning around and drawing Leo's eyes to her bum.

"No, no, it's..." Leo struggled for the right words. "It's... great, you look —"

"Help me do it up," Allissa said, showing him the open zip at the back.

Leo rose to his feet and felt his body fizz with electricity. His heart thudded. Behind his eyes, something tensed.

Reaching Allissa, Leo took a deep breath. With one hand on the base of her back, he raised the zip with the other. When it reached the top, he put both his hands on her shoulders.

"It looks," he said, turning his head to look at her reflection in the hallway mirror. "Amazing. You look amazing."

"Thanks," Allissa said, raising her right hand to his left. Their fingers intertwined.

Leo looked at them in the mirror. Him standing behind Allissa, her body pressing back into his. Allissa's eyes were large and dark and seemed to be gazing at him too.

"Do you think it'll be alright for the party?"

"I think..." Leo's pulse quickened. It was beating for them both now. He lent leant in towards Allissa's exposed neck. His chest tightened. But this was not panic. This was something more. Something instinctive. Something beautiful. Narrowing his eyes, Leo took in the beautiful slenderness of her neck. The smell of her coconut body lotion. His right hand slipped across the top of her chest.

"I think... it's perfect," he said, just an inch from her skin. Leo drew another deep breath. This was it. He had no idea what this meant, but this was good.

A harsh electronic buzz sprang from the phone by the door.

"That thing works?" Allissa said, shaking her head and stepping forward.

"Must do," Leo said, letting his breath go slowly. *They'll go away,* he thought, the words not making it to his lips. His hands dropped to his sides.

"I'll go," Allissa said, crossing to the phone. "Hello?" She paused and listened. "Hello?" she said again. The phone on the wall continued to buzz.

"Can you go and see who it is? It might be important. I'll get changed."

Leo sank into a stoop and headed for the door.

11

"What do you want to tell me then?" Olezka asked.

Keal slumped in the chair with his hands tied behind his back. Konstantin's body had been dragged from the room, leaving a dark splatter of congealing blood by Keal's feet.

"Honestly, Dedushka Olezka, I have no idea what you are talking about." Keal rolled his shoulders. They were already getting stiff from the lack of movement. "I was just having a night with a woman, and you came in and brought me here."

Olezka stopped pacing and looked at Keal. The pistol was stuffed beneath his belt and his gloved hands hung by his sides. Dull morning light from one of the cracked and grime-covered windows patterned across his face.

"It's not about what you were doing last night." Olezka's voice rumbled.

Keal's eyebrows raised. Had the mafia boss finally lost the plot?

Olezka had been running the large and dangerous

organisation for over thirty years. Keal had worked closely alongside him for a long time. He respected Olezka. In many ways, Olezka had become like a father figure to him. That's why the men called him Dedushka Olezka — *Grandfather Olezka.* Maybe the pressure had finally caught up with him. It was bound to happen at some point.

Behind Olezka, another man walked into the room. Before he had even emerged from the shadows of the corridor, Keal recognised him. Borya. Like Keal himself, Borya was high up in Olezka's organisation. Keal and Borya had joined at about the same time and were like brothers in command. Keal felt himself exhale with relief. If anyone could help Olezka see reason, it would be Borya.

"What's going on?" Borya asked, his grey-blue eyes noticing Keal's blood-splattered body.

"Borya," Keal said, "Dedushka Olezka has made a mistake —"

Keal was silenced by a flick of the leader's palm.

"Borya," Olezka said, his voice a rumble. "This man, who we've both known for many years. This man, who I have brought into our family. He has stolen from us."

"Dedushka Olezka, no way." Keal was shocked, his voice raised. "I haven't stolen anything. What am I supposed to have stolen?"

"Who's job is it to collect the shipments from the shop in Kreuzberg?" Olezka asked. "One of the most trusted jobs in the entire organisation. Who's job is it?"

Keal swallowed and felt the muscles in his shoulders begin to strain.

"That's my job Dedushka Olezka. I have done that for over a year. Every week without fail."

"Yes, you have," Olezka said, nodding slowly. "But you

see, that's the problem. I spoke with our friends in Lima. Last month they sent forty-five packages."

Keal nodded. His thick tongue licked his crusted lips.

"But we only have a record of receiving twenty-nine. So, I'll ask you again." Olezka drew the gun from his waistband and stepped across to Keal. "Is there something you want to tell me?" He placed the gun against the top of Keal's knee. Keal knew that from there, the bullet would pass behind his kneecap and shred every crucial part of his lower leg. It was a threat he'd used himself on multiple occasions.

"I... I..." Keal stuttered, his eyes looking wildly around the room. "I took all the packages that were there. I wouldn't steal. Never."

Borya watched the man's panic. He said nothing.

"I have —"

Keal's words were cut short by the faint thump of a silenced gunshot.

12

"Are you Leo Keane?"

Leo heard the question before he'd even opened the door. He saw the faint outline of a person through the frosted glass although he couldn't make out their features.

When he heard his name, Leo paused. His anxiety fluttered. His chest became tighter, and his breathing short.

How did this person know who he was? How had they found his address?

"I'm sorry to intrude," came the male voice again. A soft, well-spoken voice. "I urgently need to speak with you."

Leo shut his eyes, inhaled deeply, then coughed. His anxiety subsided with the influx of oxygen. During some periods of his life — such as after Mya's disappearance — his anxiety rendered him incapable of even leaving the house. But during other times, such as the last few months — other than the occasional surge — it seemed to have left him alone.

Letting the anxiety drift, Leo opened the door.

"Are you Leo Keane?" the man asked again. He was a

short, mousy man, probably no older than Leo. He wore a baggy jumper which might have been in service since the Second World War.

"Yes," Leo replied, trying to hide the shakiness from his voice.

"I'm... I'm sorry to accost you like this," the man said meekly. "I need to speak with you as a matter of urgency. It concerns my brother. He's missing and... I... I..."

Ten minutes later, Leo and Allissa sat opposite the man as he introduced himself as Charles Rolleston.

"I'm... I'm... sorry to, you know, take your time up like this," Charles said, warming his hands on the mug of black coffee. "I wouldn't if it wasn't urgent. I just..."

"It's alright," Allissa said, "you just need to tell us what's happened, then we'll see if we can help."

Charles took what they all hoped would be a restorative sip of coffee and grimaced at the heat and bitter taste.

"It's my brother Minty." The words came out like a torrent. "He lives in Berlin. He's a fashion designer. He has a little shop there. Sells strange clothes to rich people," — Charles looked at the hoodies Leo and Allissa wore — "nothing you or I would wear, I think."

Allissa had pulled on a large hoodie and rolled up the sleeves. Leo glanced at her and suspected it might have once belonged to him.

Allissa encouraged Charles with a nod.

"Well, then, at 4 am on Sunday morning," Charles continued, "he tried to call me. I was asleep at the time, so he left a message." Charles dug through a pocket and pulled out a smartphone. He pressed the screen a few times and laid it on the coffee table.

"Charlie, it's me," came a voice from the phone. The brothers had the same upper-class English drawl. "Listen,

I'm so sorry about this. It's... it's... things really aren't good." The voice got louder, competing with a rumble on the line. "I just want you to know that things aren't always as they seem to be, and not to lose faith in me." Then the rumble grew until it was nothing more than distortion. If Minty had said anything more, Leo couldn't make it out. After a final crackle, the phone went dead.

Charles blinked. Jewels formed in his long, dark lashes.

"The police say he jumped in front of a train." Charles' prominent Adam's apple bobbed in his thin neck.

"Take your time," Allissa said, "there's no rush. We're here to listen."

Charles put his cup on the table and dropped his head between his hands. He sucked air through thin fingers.

"I'm sorry, I'm sorry," he said, regaining control and looking up at Leo and Allissa. "It's just, I don't think he would've done that — that message. 'Things aren't as they seem. Don't lose faith.' It's just —"

"Yes, that doesn't sound like something someone would say before..." Allissa trailed off. "What about his body? Surely there would —"

"That's the thing. The authorities have told us to wait. We have the police report. But until we have the body —" Charles sobbed bitterly. Leo and Allissa could do nothing but watch.

"I just don't believe... I can't believe..." Charles took a moment to compose himself, finally looking up at the pair. "I don't know what's happened, but that's not him. I know that for sure."

13

Keal writhed and kicked with his good leg as blood pooled around him. Borya leant against the wall and watched. He tried to look calm as Keal's shrieks of pain echoed through the building.

Borya knew that Keal would die if they didn't stop the bleeding soon.

Externally Borya worked hard to appear relaxed, but inside his pulse raged. He had hoped Olezka wouldn't even notice the missing shipments. They received so many — often multiple times a day — that he doubted Olezka even kept records. Especially with the incriminating nature of such records. Borya had been wrong. He pushed his hands in his pockets so no one would see them shaking.

"Dedushka Olezka, you need to see this," Semion said, rushing past Borya and showing Olezka something on the screen of a laptop.

"Tell me," Olezka barked.

"It's the man from the shop — Minty Rolleston — he jumped in front of a U-Bahn train just a few hours ago."

"It was him. He did it!" Keal shouted between gasps. His movements were becoming weaker.

Olezka looked at Keal with eyes like the twin barrels of a shotgun.

"What, he steals shipments worth a million euros and then kills himself? Who would do that? Get this checked out," Olezka barked at Semion, "and get him patched up." He pointed a gloved hand at Keal.

Semion tied Keal's good leg to the chair to stop his writhing and then tightened a strap around his wounded one to slow the bleeding. Keal leaned back weakly. He was fighting for each breath now. His eyes roamed the room without focusing.

Olezka grabbed Keal's chin with a gloved hand. "You are still alive, that is good for you. There are two ways this will go now —"

"Help me. Help me," Keal said. A string of drool ran from his lips and into the puddle of blood.

"Yes, I could help you. I could have Semion drop you outside the hospital now. You may never use that leg again." Olezka prodded the blood-soaked leg with his finger. Keal cried in pain. "But they would probably save your life."

"Please, yes, please."

"But why would I do that?" Olezka stood up. Keal fell forward against his bindings. "You have done nothing to help me. You have stolen from me. If you admit that and tell me where the missing shipments are, then maybe you can go."

"I... I..." Keal gasped.

"Let me make this even clearer for you," Olezka said. "As you know, Semion has a bit of a talent for this persuading business. I am very basic. A bull in a shop of china. But he is much more effective. He uses drugs and blades and all sorts of things I haven't got the patience for. If you don't give me something soon, I'm sure he will be happy to take over."

Borya turned to face Semion and saw a look of pleasure flicker across his face.

The sick bastard.

14
———

As the flat's flimsy door clunked back into place behind Charles, Allissa knew what they needed to do. They would go to Berlin and find out what had happened to Charles' brother.

Climbing the stairs again, Allissa felt the relaxation of their time in Abu Dhabi evaporating. The first few hours of an investigation were the hardest. There were the logistics to organise — like transport and accommodation — and a lot of research to do. The better they knew the missing person, and the more they could get inside their mind, the easier it would be when they were on the ground in a foreign city. They needed to think like that person in order to understand where they might go.

Back in the front room, Allissa grabbed her laptop, sank into the sofa and thumbed the power button. As the computer loaded, she looked up at the empty room. An hour ago, she'd been trying on her dress for a party she now wasn't going to attend. With that thought, her right hand slid to her left shoulder. That was where her fingers had intertwined with Leo's. The embrace had been unexpected, but Allissa had liked it. Watching their reflection in the mirror, Allissa saw Leo move in to kiss her neck. Instinctively, she'd bent her head to let him in. It felt good. She was ready for it. But then the door had buzzed and —

Pushing the thoughts from her mind, Allissa opened an internet browser and typed "Minty Rolleston" into the search bar.

"As Charles told us, Minty runs this fashion website," Allissa said, turning the screen of her laptop to face Leo as he walked into the room carrying two mugs of steaming coffee. "Unusual clothes. All very expensive."

Leo had just been to the shop to get milk. They now had work to do, so proper coffee, with milk, was essential.

Leo sat down next to Allissa. He was careful to leave a space between them.

"He also has a shop in Berlin," Allissa said, "so that would be the first place to look. Just to see if anything's going on there. I've also found the address of his flat and had a look through social media at the other places he likes to go. I'll put a list together."

"Got a picture?" Leo asked, taking a sip of the coffee.

"I'll find one." Allissa tapped at the keyboard.

A few seconds later, Minty's picture appeared. Minty looked as Alissa expected: long hair ran across the shoulders of a maroon blazer, a white shirt was open at the neck to highlight a tangle of chains and pendants, and a large, dark beard contrasted super-white teeth.

"This was taken at an awards night in Milan a few weeks ago," Allissa said, reading the description. "Minty posted it on his social media. Could be worth finding out who he went with."

"Yes, good idea, you've made a good start." Leo raised the coffee to his lips.

"Well, it's not often we get a case this early. Normally people come to us weeks after the person's gone missing. We've got a great opportunity here."

Leo nodded.

"If we can move quickly here, I reckon we've got a good chance," Allissa said. "I'll have a look at flights now. We should be able to get out there tomorrow morning."

Leo put the cup down and grabbed his laptop from the bag beside him.

"No wait," he said, "you've got Lucy's party tomorrow. You've got the dress and everything."

"I'll cancel it." Allissa looked at Leo. "I'll tell her something came up."

"No, you can't. You won't. You need to go to that party. We talked about how it was your way back into the family. You need to go."

Allissa glanced from Leo to the computer. On the screen, a list of flights from London to Berlin began to load.

"Fine," Allissa said, looking back at him. "We could both go the following day. Get an early flight the morning after the party."

"Yes," Leo said thoughtfully, "although, as you say, we've got the advantage of time with this one. It would be a shame to waste even one day. I can go ahead tomorrow, and you can join me the day after."

Allissa's mouth moved to argue, but no words came out.

"I'll get some of the groundwork done," Leo said. "Start looking around and see what I find."

Without comment, Allissa made changes to the flight details on her computer. Leo could get started on his own, Allissa knew that. He had gone to Kathmandu alone. But things were different now; he didn't need to go on his own. They did things together. That's how it worked.

Sitting back, Allissa found her hand rising to the place their fingers had intertwined.

"Are you sure?" She said, turning to look at Leo. "One day won't make *that* much difference. We could just go together and —"

"Sure, yes, of course, I can do this," Leo said. "The first few hours are crucial. If we don't go now, we might not ever... you know, find out."

"Alright," Allissa said. "I'll get you a flight booked for tomorrow, and I'll join you the following day."

"Okay," Leo replied, an uncontrollable smile breeding across his face. "Although I'll probably have it solved by then. All you ever do is slow me down."

A flash of movement.

"Hey, watch out!" he shouted as Allissa elbowed him in the ribs. "I'll spill this!"

15

Borya stepped out into the bright sunshine and gulped a greedy breath of the fresh afternoon air. Surrounded by a dirty canal and the backs of some warehouses, the place felt isolated. He stood and listened to the air. The wind tickled through the thicket of trees behind the building and water splashed faintly from the canal. The sun was high in the sky now. It was turning out to be another bright Berlin day.

Borya was tired. He wasn't often up this early. But when Olezka called, you came. That was the way it worked.

Borya walked towards three cars parked in the small yard. Olezka's Rolls Royce, a black Jeep and Borya's dark blue Mercedes. The concrete was buckled with age and nature. New shoots of green clung to the cracks like a rash. Borya fumbled the keys from his pocket and unlocked the Mercedes. Opening the passenger door, he leant in and took his pipe from the glove box. Borya knew he was the only man younger than seventy to smoke a pipe, but he liked it. The process of stuffing it with tobacco and the cool taste of the smoke was far better than cigarettes and cigars.

Leaning on the fender, Borya looked up at the building. It had that sort of old-worldly charm that was common in Berlin's decrepit structures. A kind of natural wonkiness, a softness on the eye. Borya thought modern designers would do well to copy and replicate it.

A bird called from somewhere in the undergrowth behind the building. Another answered a few seconds later.

Borya drew the pouch of tobacco from inside his coat. His hands had almost stopped shaking; that was good. The problem was, the thing that made him nervous was that Keal had seen him with Minty at the shop a few weeks ago. Borya had gone by to check things over, just to make sure Minty was doing what they'd asked. It was stupid, he shouldn't have been there, but he just wanted to make sure things were alright. He'd even got a friend to drive him there so no one would see his car outside. It was just bad luck for Keal to arrive at the same time. It was just bad luck. But Borya had no business being at the shop that day, and if Olezka found out he had been there...

Borya felt a rancid taste bubble into his mouth. He spat it to the floor.

He just had to hope that Keal thought nothing of it. Borya knew that if his being there was questioned, then Olezka may arrive at an entirely different conclusion.

"No, no, no, no!" The yelled words echoed from the bowels of the dilapidated building. Two pigeons resting on one of the old windowsills thumped into the air.

Borya had worked with Olezka for a long time and knew his patience was limited. If Keal didn't come up with something soon, a bullet in the brain would seem like a holiday.

Borya grimaced as another scream reverberated. He hadn't intended for Olezka to blame Keal. Borya hadn't thought Olezka would find out at all. There were so many packages. He thought it would be impossible for Olezka to account for them all. Borya had obviously underestimated the *Vor v Zakone*.

With an unsteady hand, Borya tapped out the old tobacco from the pipe and began to repack it. His hands shook as he pressed the leaves into the bowl with his thumb.

"It's a messy business," came a guttural voice from the doorway. Borya fumbled with the pipe and tobacco scattered to the concrete. Olezka crossed the yard.

"That man, though." Olezka pointed back towards the building. "He has to know something. It's the only way. I've no idea how long he's been doing it for. *Ublyudok.*"

Borya lifted the pipe with both hands, clenched it firmly between his teeth, and rummaged through his coat pockets for a lighter.

"You need a light? Let me." Olezka took a lighter from the pocket of his jacket. He still wore his gloves.

"Thanks," Borya said. There was a bloody stain on the lighter's glinting surface.

"No, not this. Please no. Noooo!" echoed across the yard. Olezka didn't react at all. Borya took a deep drag on the pipe.

"If he knows anything," Olezka said, "Semion will get it out of him."

Borya nodded. He hoped never to know what Semion did to people. He had seen grown men turn into babies after two hours with Semion.

"I didn't want to do this, you understand." Olezka turned to face Borya.

Borya nodded and felt the impact of Olezka's dark stare.

"I am sad to see it happen. You and Keal have been like sons to me. I just can't have people stealing from me."

"I understand, Dedushka Olezka," Borya said. He took another drag on the pipe. "Anyone would do the same."

The older man nodded. "Hey Borya, you don't look so good. Are you feeling alright?" Olezka's voice lightened.

"Anything, I'll do anything! No!" The pitiful begging resonated through the empty rooms of the derelict building.

"Yes, I'm alright," Borya replied. "Just tired. A lot of work lately."

"I understand." Olezka put a gloved hand on Borya's forearm. "You go home and get some rest now. You don't need to be here. I'll come and see you later."

"Thank you, I will," Borya said.

Olezka turned and walked back towards the building.

Borya looked down at the place where Olezka's gloved hand had rested. A deep red stain was now soaking into the fabric.

16

Willing herself to wake up, Allissa closed her eyes tight until the colours danced. She opened them again slowly and looked through the window of the train. Outside, the darkened countryside of West Sussex rolled past beneath the milky glow of the pre-dawn sky.

The previous night had been a late one. They'd stayed up to book flights, trains, and read all the information they could find on Minty and his supposed death. They'd received the police report from Charles which, with the help of an online translator, detailed that at 5 am, a man who was later identified as Minty Rolleston was killed in an incident at Kottbusser Tor U-Bahn station. The police were not treating the death as suspicious or unusual. The event had not even been mentioned in the local press. Maybe the death of a British ex-patriot was not particularly newsworthy.

In a few minutes, Leo would be getting off the train at Gatwick Airport, from where he would fly alone to Berlin. Allissa was continuing on to London, where she'd get a connecting train to Reading for the party this evening. Allissa blinked again. She hadn't needed to get up this early, but something had made her want to travel with Leo. It felt like being involved.

"Go straight to the train station where it happened," Allissa said, suppressing a yawn, "Kottbusser Tor U-Bahn."

"That's what I plan to do," Leo replied without looking up from his phone.

"Then maybe to the shop. If anything looks dangerous —"

"Yes, I know," Leo said, grinning, "I'll wait for you. Honestly, it's going to be fine. I'm just going to get a load of the boring groundwork done. You won't miss any of the fun, I promise."

Allissa forced a smile. She didn't like the thought of Leo going on his own. She knew first-hand that their line of work was dangerous. Anything could happen in the next twenty-four hours.

Allissa tensed as a computerised voice reminded them that London Gatwick was the next stop. Sure, she wanted to reconnect with her family, but over the last few months she and Leo had done everything together. Good, bad and dangerous — they'd faced it all, side by side.

"I could just come with you now," she blurted out. "Don't worry about the party. I'm sure they'll understand."

"No," Leo said evenly. "You're going to the party. You need to see your family. I'll be fine."

"But what if —"

"I told you, nothing's going to happen. I'll just be doing the boring stuff until you get there." Leo slid his hand across the table and placed it over hers. "It's going to be fine."

Allissa nodded against her swelling discomfort.

The computerised voice confirmed they were now approaching London Gatwick. Leo rose to his feet.

"Remember you need to keep me updated," Allissa said. "I want to know everything."

"I will," Leo said, slinging his bag across his shoulder. "Remember you can watch my progress on that new app thingy too."

They'd installed a new app on both their phones which allowed them to see each other's location. Leo hadn't been sure about it at first, but Allissa insisted.

As Allissa nodded, her stomach tightened further.

"I'll be there tomorrow afternoon," Allissa said. "I've got the address of the hotel, but I imagine you'll be out by then so let me know where to meet you."

"Don't worry." Leo rested his hand on Allissa's shoulder. "I'll get the boring stuff done today. Don't worry about me. You need to enjoy this party."

"I will," Allissa lied. "I'll see you tomorrow." Then, without thinking, she stood and hugged Leo tight. Leo put his arms around her too.

The train pulled to a stop and the doors buzzed. A few sleepy passengers began to move.

"You need to go," Allissa said, breaking off the hug.

"Yep," Leo said, stepping backwards. "See you tomorrow."

Through the window, Allissa watched Leo pull his backpack tight and head for the exit. As the train started to move, she looked away. She would be there tomorrow. It was just a few hours. But regardless of the time, somewhere within her, a sense of deep foreboding grew unbidden.

17

Anafisa fought for breath as the man's thick hands closed around her neck. She felt each finger tightening, constricting, extinguishing. She felt each individual muscle pushing down on her throat. She grabbed at his wrists, but they didn't move. Beneath his cold skin, the muscles pulled tighter. She scratched at his face. One of her dazzling nails caught his shaved head. It was cold and hard, like marble.

He lengthened his arms and pushed her against the wall. She thudded to the plaster. Two paintings fell. Glass smashed across the floor. He shoved her again. Anafisa felt the last bit of air leave her lungs.

"You have two options," he grunted in their native Russian. "I'm coming back in one week, and I'll either be taking my money or" — his right hand released her neck and grabbed her by the wrist — "I'll be taking one of these pretty fingers for each ten-thousand you owe me."

Anafisa felt the floor rush up to meet her as the man let her go. She took several greedy breaths then opened her eyes.

Anafisa shot up in the bed. The sheets, tangled around her writhing body, were wet from sweat. She was breathless. She looked around. She wasn't at home, but she was alone.

That was unusual. It was unlike Keal to get up early. Anafisa pushed herself up in the bed and let her breathing subside. She had dreamt about the man's visit for the last four nights. She had three days to find his money.

Anafisa reached to the bedside table and picked up her handbag. Her clothes were strewn across the floor. Opening the bag, she checked the money Keal had given her last night. He had paid her well, and it hadn't even taken that long. These gangster types were all about the show. It was all about massaging their ego. They wanted to go out and look good. Hang around in some exclusive bars, drink champagne and snort cocaine. By the time they got home, they were done after a few pumps. That was if things down there were working at all by then. Either way, it didn't matter to Anafisa.

Anafisa exhaled and rubbed a hand across her neck. She counted the money again. She still didn't have enough.

She would have to sell something, after all. Her thoughts ran to her gleaming Maserati Levante parked outside. She could probably cover the debt if she sold that, but then what was she supposed to drive?

When Anafisa had moved to Berlin, she had it all going for her. She had a lump sum of money from her husband's estate, the apartment in Berlin, one in the Alps, jewellery and all the rest. She was set for life.

Where did it all go wrong?

Anafisa dropped her handbag to the bed and saw the exact reason it went wrong. It glimmered at her from the bedside table. Keal must have left it. He wouldn't mind if she had a taste. Anafisa reached over and picked up the bag of cocaine. It was a big one, a few grams at least. Normally she would smoke it, but there was no time right now. She dove a long nail expertly into the powder and brought it up to her nose. Then she inhaled, and the beasts of addiction faded away.

That was the problem. That was where it all went wrong.

But the thing was...

Anafisa settled back into the pillows.

The thing was...

Anafisa didn't know what the thing was. She couldn't remember now. Anafisa smiled as a wave of warmth shrouded her body. Whatever "the thing" was, how could it matter when she felt this good?

She closed her eyes again. Anafisa didn't even consider what the white powder had cost her. The money she'd lost. The flat she'd had to mortgage. The money she'd had to borrow from one of Berlin's most dangerous men.

Settling back in the bed, Anafisa actually thought of nothing. Anafisa loved thinking of nothing.

If she had been capable of thought, though, she would have cursed the day she'd ever met Olezka Ivankov.

18

Watching Berlin slide beneath the belly of the Boeing, Leo thought about the flight he'd taken into Kathmandu. He remembered looking out at the sprawling concrete chaos of the mountain city, and the overwhelming feeling of walking out amongst the noise, the dust and the oppressive heat.

Berlin looked different; organised and sedate. There were vast open spaces of green, wide boulevards and lazily snaking rivers. It was a city largely devoid of tall buildings, but it seemed to sprawl, calm and sensitive, into the hazy horizon. *That's reassuring,* Leo thought as he sipped from his bottle of water.

Not only was this city vastly different from Kathmandu, but *he* felt different too. Back then, he'd had no idea how to find someone in the real world. But he'd done it, and, he supposed slightly pretentiously, he'd found a stronger version of himself along the way. Of course, his anxiety was still there. It always would be. It was a part of him; like his dislike for shellfish, his knobbly knees or his inability to tolerate the music of Take That. But, thankfully, although it occasionally reared its ugly, all-encompassing head, it was no longer his mind's default setting.

His new life seemed to ground him. It gave him purpose. He loved the intensity of the research process; working hard to get into someone's personality and see things from their perspective. Despite his anxious disposition, he also loved the action of the chase. The excitement of knowing the person they were looking for was nearby. Maybe just two steps ahead. And he loved working with Allissa. They seemed to balance each other out. She had a fearless streak and pushed him out of his comfort zone, and he had a matter of fact way of thinking that brought them back down to earth. They were both passionate investigators and, Leo thought, the memory of her in the clinging black dress swimming across his mind, she was beautiful.

As the plane banked to land at Schönefeld Airport, Leo looked at the seat next to him. It was empty. He had insisted that Allissa attended the party. She'd spent two years without her family and this was her opportunity to reconnect with them. He couldn't let her miss it. Although he was looking forward to her joining him tomorrow.

19

Semion smiled as he looked at the tip of the needle. There was something so perfect about it. It was so straight and neat and flawless. Semion walked to the only window which wasn't bricked up or shaded by trees. Dust floated around him in the thick bar of light. He held up the tip of the needle. It glimmered beautifully. For a moment, Semion thought it looked heavenly. Then, turning to see the scene behind him, he realised how far from heavenly this really was.

Semion's smile widened. It might not look heavenly, but he was an artist, and this was his canvas. Most of the space was dank, dusty and colourless — the grey of flaking paint and decaying concrete. Only two things added colour to the scene; the listless scrawls of the spray can, and the blood of the man tied to the chair.

"You know this place used to be a bakery," Semion said. The man couldn't see Semion standing behind him. But he whimpered at the sound of the voice.

Maybe he's tired, Semion thought. *I'll add a bit of something to wake him up too.*

Semion took a phial from a bag at his feet, inserted the needle and pulled some into the syringe. He paused, looked at the man and grinned.

Maybe a little more. He's a big guy.

"Yes, during the Second-World-War it was used as a bakery. They used to bake forty thousand loaves of bread a day here," Semion said. He pushed the syringe until liquid sprayed from the needle. "It was all manned by people from the concentration camps. Forced labour." Semion walked up behind the man.

Keal whimpered again.

"A fantastic feat of organisation wouldn't you say? Forty thousand loaves a day."

Semion put his hand on the side of Keal's neck. Keal was too weak to even attempt to move.

"This drug I'm going to give you was also pioneered in one of those camps." Semion looked at the needle again. "It'll give me access to everything inside here." He tapped Keal's head gently then pushed the needle into his skin.

Keal twisted, but Semion held him still.

"You won't feel a thing, ever again," Semion said, sliding down the plunger.

20

After napping, showering and slipping into the black dress, Allissa applied make-up in the hotel room's full-length mirror. A playlist of cheerful music screamed from her phone which she'd stood in an empty glass for extra volume.

Having stayed in hundreds of hotels across the globe, from opulent luxury, quirky boutique and basic budget, Allissa knew there was little that depressed her more than the identical rooms of banal chain hotels. The three coat hangers drooping from the rail in the doorless wardrobe, their heads twisted around so they couldn't be removed, and the two cups upturned by a mini kettle with four tea bags, sachets of coffee and milk in a plastic cup felt like life averaged and then rounded down. The room met the needs of the occupant while stripping out any possibility of fun or unnecessary enjoyment — utilitarianism in the land of its masters.

It didn't matter to Allissa though. She was only here for a few hours, before going to the party and then off to Berlin in the morning. She took a swig from a can of pale ale. She'd bought a four-pack at Victoria Station that morning and was already on her third. She reassured herself she would need some Dutch courage for the party tonight. Glancing at her phone, she thought about Leo. He would be landing about now but hadn't yet texted back. Maybe he'd been held up. She would call him later.

Finishing the application of her make-up and making some final adjustments to her hair, Allissa appraised herself in the mirror. Her reflection didn't look like her at all. For one, she rarely wore make-up. If she did, it was subtle and not the full effort she'd gone through today. Secondly, she was used to seeing herself wearing baggy and comfortable clothes. The figure-hugging black dress was very unusual. It looked good though, she thought, her eyes roaming across her reflection.

The shoes were the next challenge. Pulling a pair of high heels from her bag, Allissa sat on the bed and looped the straps around her feet. She couldn't remember the last time she wore high-heeled shoes. She fastened the straps and stood up, then stepped tentatively over to the mirror. The length of the heels elongated her legs and extended her posture.

Allissa downed what remained of the beer. Then she grabbed her phone and snapped a picture of her reflection in the mirror.

"Ready for the party... wish me luck Xx," she typed, then sent it to Leo.

21

Leo felt confident as he followed signs from the airport to the train station. He had researched the journey last night and knew where he was going. Finding the platform, he leant back against a pillar and closed his eyes. His tired mind spun with details of the case. Further down the platform, a group of young German woman waited with their brightly coloured suitcases.

As the train approached, Leo shook himself alert and rubbed his hand across his face. He'd check into the hotel, then grab a coffee.

Leo found an empty seat, pulled off his backpack and sat down. The young women sat across the aisle from him. Their loud voices filled the otherwise empty carriage, but Leo didn't mind. He always found he enjoyed hearing people speak in languages he didn't understand. The same group speaking English would have irritated him, but the unknown language seemed to drift past.

Leo rubbed his face again and forced himself to look away from the empty seat opposite him. The flat industrial landscape of Berlin's outskirts drifted past the window.

After a few minutes it became more densely packed. Modern buildings in glass and chrome fought for attention next to Soviet-era monoliths and ornate nineteenth-century domes. The closer they got to the city, the more varied, jumbled and exciting the architecture became. Changing trains at Ostkreuz, Leo headed in the direction of the city centre. He was almost there. Two stops later, beneath the grand canopy of Ostbahnhof, he headed for the street.

With the help of the map on his phone, Leo found the brutalist concrete building his hotel occupied and checked in quickly. He climbed the stairs to his room on the sixth floor and thought about the hotel he'd stayed at in Kathmandu. Things there were just so different. Even getting a taxi there had been difficult. But, Leo realised, looking at the map on the screen of the phone, he was better prepared now.

Unlocking the door, Leo stepped inside. The room was decorated in sixties-style green and yellow wallpaper. On the far wall hung an oversized picture of a middle-aged man. The image was so large that Leo felt he could see each pore and hair on the man's oily skin. The label beneath the picture told him the gentleman had been the German Democratic Republic's Minister for Fishing. Leo leaned back on his heels and frowned. He liked learning about a place, but the long-dead eyes of the German Democratic Republic's Minister for Fishing made him uncomfortable.

Leo turned away and dropped his bag on the bed. Then he pulled out a slip of euros, swapped them for the pounds in his wallet and checked his phone. A message from Allissa was waiting.

"Ready for the party... wish me luck, Xx."

Leo closed the message. He would reply when he had

something to tell her. He slid the phone back into his pocket, then turned and left the room.

Half an hour later as he descended the stairs at Kottbusser Tor U-Bahn station, one question revolved around Leo's mind: could this be the place where Minty Rolleston ended his own life?

Leo knew he was unlikely to find any physical evidence of Minty's death at the station but wanted to see the place to try and understand why a young and successful man might throw himself in front of a train. The first thing Leo needed to figure out, and as quickly as possible, was whether Minty was actually dead or not. If Minty was dead, then sooner or later his remains would be released. That would be all the proof anyone needed. This may just be a case of the authorities taking their time. If so, then he and Allissa could do nothing to help. Leo knew that suicides happened with horrific frequency, leaving families shredded with anguish.

He had thought it unusual there wasn't more from the police though. The report had been so simple and promised no further investigation. Then there was the lack of information about the body. Surely if there were no questions to be answered, the body could be released immediately? So why then were the police being so secretive?

With these thoughts circling like greedy vultures, Leo looked around the platform. Where moments before, he had ridden on a bright yellow train between the chaotic and colourful roofs of Kreuzberg, now there seemed to be no colour in anything. The fluorescent overhead lights bleached the station's grey tiles and withered the faces of the solemn commuters. Leo looked at a woman who was probably in her thirties but had ten years added to her appearance by the bleak lighting.

Leo walked down the platform and looked around. He

had no real idea of what he was looking for — just something, anything that sparked his interest.

A macabre thought slipped into Leo's mind — what a horrible place to die. In a city of colour, intrigue and excitement, what a bland and dreary corner to choose to be your last.

22

Attacking someone's body is such an animalistic way to get them to talk, Semion thought as he watched the man's face strain beneath the ravages of the drug.

Going to their brain was a much more direct route. That's where the memories were kept. That's where a man's true strength was. No man, regardless of his physical strength, his intelligence or his experience, could fight the effect of potent psychosomatic drugs.

Semion sat on another metal chair opposite Keal. A video camera on a tripod recorded Keal's every move and sound. Semion felt that what he was doing here was science. It was his duty to document his work.

He looked down at the clipboard on which he'd written the questions he was going to ask. Semion planned to check what Keal said against the record of packages Olezka had received.

Semion knew that the interrogation needed to be conducted systematically. He had to build a hypothesis and then test it with repetitive questioning.

Semion crouched in front of Keal. He leant in until he could feel the man's breath on his face. With his left hand on Keal's chin to steady the rocking, Semion used two fingers to lift Keal's eyelids. The pupils were dilated and unfocused.

"Excellent," Semion said, "I think we are ready for our little chat."

Semion pulled the chair closer to Keal and sat. With the man in this state, Semion was in no danger. Keal's brain would be moving at light speed, even though on the surface all appeared to be still.

"Keal," Semion said, his voice low and resonant, "I want you to tell me about your visit to pick up the packages from Minty's shop yesterday."

"Yesterday. Yes." Keal's voice was compliant, measured and slow. "I went to the shop. Minty wasn't there, so I let myself in with my key. Everything was normal. I collected the four packages that had arrived in the last four days."

Semion checked that against the information Olezka had given him. It was correct. Keal had also handed four packages to Olezka. Semion noted that down.

"Thank you, Keal. You're doing really well. Now tell me about the time before. When was that, and what happened then?"

Keal's jaw ground ferociously, and his head shook. Then he began to speak.

"That was five days ago. I got to the shop and Minty was there. He was unhappy about something. I'm not sure what. He barely even spoke to me. I picked up the packages and left. There were five of them. Four small and one bigger."

Semion checked the notes. Again, the man was correct. He wrote that down.

Maybe Olezka has got this wrong.

"And the time before that?" Semion asked.

Keal's eyes fluttered and focused for a second before descending back into the thick haze of the drugs.

"That was four days before. I arrived as normal. The shop was open already, so I just walked in. I was running late. Minty was there. He was talking to someone out the back. I picked up the packages —"

"How many were there?"

"There were six packages. Two big and four small."

Semion checked the notes. Correct.

"I was just about to leave when I saw the person Minty was talking to walk from the backroom and into the shop. It was Borya."

Keal's words slurred to a stop.

Semion's eyes shot up.

Keal's head lolled forwards.

"What did you just say?" Semion asked.

Keal muttered something unintelligible.

"Keal, take me through that visit to the shop again."

Keal's body shook and then went limp.

23

When looking for someone, Leo had learned to rely on his feelings and instincts. They told him where to look, what to accept as truth and what to challenge. Right now, he had a feeling things weren't fitting together as they should.

Minty was a bright, colourful and vibrant man. A man with a successful business. A man who lived his life to excess — not one who, Leo thought, would choose to end it in a place like this. Sure, maybe his private and public personas were different. But then, would he really have ended his life in such a public way?

The rumble of an approaching train overwhelmed the white noise hum of the station. Leo turned to face the dark eye of the tunnel. Warm air buffeted him. As a light appeared, Leo felt the vibrations climb through his feet. A moment later, the yellow body of the train leapt into the station. With a hiss of brakes, it started to slow. The train was still going fast when it reached Leo halfway down the platform.

Fast enough... Leo shuddered.

The train eased to a stop, and its doors buzzed open. Half a dozen passengers stepped out and headed for the exit. Leo stepped away from the waiting train and looked down at his phone. Pushing in one of his earphones, he played the voicemail message he'd recorded from Charles' answerphone. Beneath Minty's words was the same gushing rattle of the arriving train.

In a staccato of ascending gears, the train began to accelerate from the station.

As the train's rumble faded to silence, Leo listened to the recording again. This time he counted the seconds between the start of the noise and the end of the recording. Six seconds. He counted again. Yes, there were six seconds between the sound of the train entering the station and the end of the recording — the impact.

Hearing the rumble of the next train approaching, Leo stood ready. First, the darkness of the tunnel was solid. Then a single light pierced the darkness. Then the rails began to glisten.

Leo watched, waiting, ready to count.

As the train lurched into the station with the whining of engines and hissing of brakes, Leo counted. One, two, three, four... and then the train passed him. Leo continued counting. It was six seconds to the final pillar. Eight, and the train finally pulled to a stop.

Seven seconds was approximately the halfway point between the final pillar and the wall. It wasn't an exact science, Leo knew that, but it might give him an estimation of where Minty was on the platform. That could be helpful. Right now, anything could be helpful.

Leo walked to the point where he estimated Minty had

made the call. It was about three-quarters of the way along the platform.

The doors slid closed, and the train began to glide from the station. Leo would be ready for it when the next train arrived. He would listen to the recording, and if the sounds matched up, then he was in the right place.

Leo felt his phone vibrate in his hand. An icon showed the receipt of a message. Leo jabbed it impatiently, and a message filled the screen. Leo didn't need the interruptions right now. Seeing it was from Allissa, he felt an irrational prickle of irritation.

Doesn't she think I can do this on my own?

"What do you think? Xx." The message said. There was a picture attached.

Leo thumbed the button, and an image filled the screen. In the photo, Allissa was wearing the dress she had tried on yesterday, but now she wore makeup and high-heeled shoes. For a moment too long, Leo found himself looking at the impossible slenderness of her waist, the bulge of the hips, and her legs, lengthened by the shoes. Her skin glowed even more flawlessly than usual, and her hair tumbled in great curls beside her face. Leo remembered their embrace. The feeling of her body beside his. They'd known each other a long time now and had spent hundreds, maybe even thousands of hours together, but was this something else?

"What do you think?"

What did he think? Leo couldn't explain it but found himself grinning. With the noise of the train fading into the whispering tunnel, Leo looked up.

What did he think? Allissa was a beautiful woman. She looked great. His frown dissolved, and he wished he was there just to see her like that.

Dejected, Leo looked down at the tracks.
She just looked, just... How could he...
Then, through the mist of his thoughts, Leo saw something on the rails where a young man was supposed to have ended his life.

24

Borya's eyes shot open as the sound of a car approached on the road outside. That was surely Olezka coming with his men. Borya would soon be the one tied to the chair in an abandoned building. As the rumble of the car's engine passed and faded back into the city, Borya felt himself breathe again.

Maybe Keal had forgotten all about him that day in the shop. It was only a fleeting greeting from someone he knew. Maybe he hadn't even considered it unusual. Maybe he'd forgotten about it entirely.

Borya propped himself up in the bed and looked around the room. He lived in a fashionable apartment in the Kreuzberg district. It was just a few blocks away from Minty's shop in fact. The dark wooden floors, bright white walls and luxurious furnishings of the apartment brought him no pleasure today though. All Borya could think about was Olezka, Semion and that chair in the abandoned building.

The city looked bright beyond the undrawn curtains.

Was it really so wrong that he was taking a little bit for himself and Minty?

The city was changing. Olezka wouldn't be around forever, and Borya needed to make sure he was protected. It was just looking after Number One — no one could blame him for that.

The electronic grunt of the door entry system snapped Borya from his thoughts. Who was that? With his heart in his throat, Borya rose from the bed and padded through the apartment. He picked up the entry system's receiver. The black and white screen flickered into life.

Borya held onto the door frame for support. He felt dizzy. Bile raged in his stomach. The screen showed Olezka waiting outside.

"Borya." The phone strained with the low rumble of the boss's voice. "How are you feeling?"

"Yes, better," Borya replied.

Had he been rumbled? He can't have been. If the boss knew, he would come silently in the middle of the night. He wouldn't be ringing the doorbell. This was just a social call.

His heart thronging in his ears, Borya pressed the door release button and watched the screen as Olezka stepped inside.

"It's just all this stuff this morning has got me thinking. I need more people I can trust. I've been doing this too long."

Olezka and Borya stood in the kitchen. Borya had offered drinks, but the boss had declined.

"Things are changing, and we need to keep up." Olezka's dark eyes locked on Borya. "Maybe I'm too old to notice these things anymore. There must have been signs that this was going on."

"I didn't notice anything," Borya said, jamming his

hands in his pockets to stop them moving with nervous energy.

"It's my job to notice things like that. But maybe I've been doing this too long. Borya, I want you to step up and take over some of the operations for me."

25

Scanning the rails, Leo saw a flash of light. A spark of something reflective. It may just be a mirror or a piece of glass lying on the oil-stained gravel. But perhaps it was something more important than that. Leo needed to get a better look.

Leo looked around. Suddenly, he felt conscious that someone might be watching him. Footsteps echoed from the stairs as the final passengers headed towards the street. The platform was empty.

Leo walked to the platform's edge and stared down at the rails. He narrowed his eyes. Whatever it was, it was almost indistinguishable from the gravel. He could only see it when it reflected in the bleak overhead lights. Leo stepped from side to side and watched to see if it would catch the light again. He hoped no one was looking at him — this would definitely make him appear unhinged.

There it was again, a flash from the dark gravel.

Leo dropped into a squat on the platform's edge and the thing flashed again. Leo leant forward, trying to make out the shape. If it was a piece of glass or some reflective rubbish, then he could move on.

It flashed again. This time it was clear. Leo was sure of what he saw now. On the oil-saturated gravel, its screen cracked and dulled, lay a phone.

Of course, it could be anyone's phone. There was nothing to suggest it was Minty's. But it was a coincidence, and Leo knew that coincidences needed to be looked at very carefully.

Hearing the distant rumble of another approaching train, Leo took a step backwards. There was a phone on the tracks where Minty had supposedly fallen. The feeling Leo had tamed as he entered the station grew. Something here wasn't right.

A woman carrying a small dog descended the stairs and watched Leo curiously. He didn't even notice as he stood deep in thought.

Leo unlocked his phone as he heard the rumble of an approaching train. He needed to hear the recording again, just to be sure he was in the right place.

Minimising the picture of Allissa in the dress, Leo selected the audio player and waited. He would reply to Allissa later. Right now, he needed to focus on this. His thumb hovered above the play button. Leo watched the dark mouth of the tunnel as it began to lighten. First, the single pinprick of light. Then the reflection on the sweeping rails. Then, as the train's yellow front filled the tunnel's opening, Leo pressed play. Minty's voice came through the earpiece. The roaring engines. Whining brakes. The thunder of steel on steel. Leo could repeat Minty's message word for word.

"Charlie, it's me... I'm so sorry about this..."

The noise grew in the station and on the recording — the hiss of breaks.

"It's... it's... things really aren't good..."

The whine of the slowing electric motors.

"Don't lose faith in me..."

The train rushed towards him, both on the recording and in the station.

There was a crash. The earpiece went silent.

The train groaned to a stop, and the doors slid open. Leo stepped out of the way of the few people making their way out. His mind barely registered their movement. He was still thinking of the implications of what he'd discovered — the timing on the recording matched the real train entering the station. This was where Minty had supposedly collided with the train.

As the departing train accelerated away in the now-familiar rush of wind and noise, Leo shook himself back into the present. There was a phone on the tracks right here. That was too much of a coincidence.

The final passengers made their way towards the street and a quiet settled over the station. Leo glanced at the arrivals board. The next train wouldn't be here for a full five minutes. Leo looked around at the empty platform. He knew what he needed to do.

26

"Keal, come back to me. This is important," Semion said.

The man didn't respond.

Semion swore, leant forward and slapped Keal hard around the face. His head swayed with the impact, then became still.

Semion swore again. He checked Keal's neck for a pulse. It was weak but he was definitely still alive. He would need another dose. The problem was, the more he had, the less chance there was he would recover.

Semion dug his phone out and called Olezka. He needed to check this through.

"I, WELL... I..." Borya stuttered.

Olezka wanted him to take over some of their operations. This was a big deal. He felt himself smile.

A shrill buzz pierced the silence. Olezka pulled a small, low-tech phone from his coat pocket.

"It's Semion," he said to Borya. "I must get this."

"Of course." Borya nodded.

"Why don't you get us that drink now," Olezka said, holding the phone to his ear.

Borya crossed the kitchen, collected two glasses and a bottle of vodka. He knew this was one of Olezka's favourites.

"Yes, do whatever it takes," Olezka said. "Just get it done and then... you know what to do."

———

SEMION FILLED the syringe with the same dose as last time and held it up to the light again. *No,* he thought, a grin forming, *a little more.*

When the syringe was loaded, Semion sank it into Keal's neck and pushed the plunger. Then he sat back on his chair and watched. As Keal's body began to convulse once more, Semion grinned. *This stuff worked quick.*

"Now then Keal," Semion said when the shaking had stopped. "A few days ago, you went to Minty's shop and you said Borya was there."

"Yes," Keal replied clearly.

"Can you tell me exactly what happened?"

"It was strange because when I got there, there was a car outside."

"Borya's blue Mercedes?"

"No, it was a Maserati. A red one. I'd recognize it anywhere."

Semion made a note of this.

"I went inside and picked up the stuff. Just as I was about to leave, Borya appeared from the back room. He and Minty started discussing something about the clothes Minty made.

I said hello, then got out of there. There were six packages that time."

Semion jotted the details down.

"When I left, the car was still there. Someone was sitting in the driver's seat. I didn't recognise them, though."

Semion scribbled that down as his grin became a full smile.

Borya was there. That could only mean one thing.

27

As a decent, sensible person, Leo knew there were some things you just shouldn't do. Society didn't just tell you these things; it painted a technicolour picture of what would happen if you did them. Such forbidden acts are ingrained into popular culture; the killer gets caught, the wicked witch dies, and trespassing on railways is a terrible idea.

To this day Leo remembered sitting in a damp classroom, the rain beating hard against the leaking school windows, his shoes still wet from the journey there, and being made to watch a railways safety video. It followed the true story of a young boy who had thought it a good idea to play on a railway. Like a Shakespearian tragedy, it didn't end well. He had been electrocuted and possibly died — Leo couldn't remember exactly. Maybe there had been a happy ending. Either way, the video was gruesome. The boy was shown — in a reconstruction — twitching for some time on the railway's electric line. The video taught Leo two things. Firstly, you shouldn't dick around on the tracks, and secondly, if you avoided the electric rail, you'd probably be fine.

Now looking down at the tracks of the Berlin underground system, Leo noticed they had the same setup. On the far wall, the third rail was raised higher than the other two.

Leo thought he could quite easily jump down there, get the phone and be back on the platform in less than ten seconds. A lump grew in his throat.

Leo glanced around. The platform was empty. A voice echoed from somewhere near the stairs, but its owner was out of sight. On the digital arrivals board, the five minutes until the next train ticked over to four.

Of course, there would be CCTV, but Leo thought he could probably get down there and back before anyone had the chance to respond. He estimated it would take no more than ten seconds — ten seconds to make or break this investigation.

Leo swallowed hard, stuffed his phone deep in his pocket and stepped towards the platform's edge. If that phone was Minty's, then Leo needed to see it. The truth about a young man's life or death hung in the balance.

To the left, a red signal radiated from the mouth of the tunnel. A clock on the wall counted the seconds away. To the right, the platform remained empty. The digital arrivals board said the next train would arrive in four minutes.

Leo heard the voices of passengers waiting for a train in the opposite direction. They were somewhere down the platform and obscured by pillars and signs.

Leo drew a deep breath and forced the mawkish educational safety video back into the confines of his childhood memories. Then he stepped towards the platform's edge. The seconds dropped, each jarring with the ticking of the station clock. He needed that phone. It was now or never.

Glancing left and right again, Leo took a deep breath. His chest felt tight as anxiety raged.

To be anxious now was normal, Leo assured himself. He was doing something scary. That's what anxiety was — an automatic mechanism to stop people doing dangerous things.

He rubbed a hand across his face and examined the tunnel's gaping mouth. Soon the headlight of a rushing train would occupy that void. Then the light would grow and grow, and in a few seconds, the front of the train would roar into the station.

Three minutes came and went on the digital arrivals board.

Leo looked around again. He couldn't see anyone on the platform, and he couldn't hear anything beyond his thumping pulse.

His body screamed against what he was about to do.

Do not get on the tracks.

Leo knew that once he lowered himself to the platform's edge, he would have to move quickly. Anyone who saw him would trigger an alarm. As long as he got the phone, that didn't matter.

He needed to act now.

Right now.

Leo fought to draw a deep breath. He felt the stale underground air fill his lungs. The damp heat. The scent which may have been Minty's last. It could be his last if he didn't hurry up.

Go now.

Leo clenched his teeth and dropped into a crouch. The concrete of the platform was cold beneath his hands. He counted to three and then he jumped.

The gravel crunched beneath his feet as he landed. Leo's

knees stung with the impact. Without a backwards look, he stepped towards the phone, bent down and picked it up. The phone felt greasy. Without looking at it, Leo slid it deep into his pocket. He'd have plenty of time to examine it later.

A warm front of damp air swelled from the cavernous tunnel. It surrounded Leo. It choked him. Somewhere nearby, something rumbled — metal on metal.

Leo needed to get off the rails now. He turned and stepped against the platform. As a man of average height, the platform's concrete lip was level with his waist. He placed his hands flat on the concrete. Hoisting himself back up shouldn't be difficult. Leo prepared to swing his left knee up onto the platform. Then, he heard a rumble — a force field of sound and air. The vibration knocked the breath from him. Leo turned and looked deep into the void. He heard the rumble again. Then he saw a bright pinprick of light — a star in the night sky. A train was approaching.

Tensing his muscles, Leo swung his leg up onto the platform. He needed to get off the tracks. Now!

The rumble grew. Leo's breath caught in his throat. His ankle slipped from the dusty concrete. It fell and struck the rail. Leo felt a stab of pain, sharp as a thrusted knife. He winced.

Leo felt the shuddering tonnes of the approaching train. His knees began to vibrate.

The streak of light had now become a solid, looming headlight.

The distant rumble — the rumour of movement elsewhere — had become a roar.

Leo stepped up on to the rail. He felt the approaching train thundering through the steel.

Pushing himself up, Leo swung his legs and rolled onto the platform.

Berlin

His breath stung, and his ankle throbbed.
The train roared into the station. Brakes screamed.
Leo lay on his back on the platform. He had the phone.

28

For Minty, being dead really was frustrating. Where he'd usually be able to go to the shops on a bright afternoon or meet friends for drinks, now he was confined to the house.

It wasn't as bad as actually being dead, he supposed, as it was only for a couple of days. So it was definitely a lot better than being medically dead. Death being, well, permanent.

But the days were seeming very long indeed. He couldn't go out. Couldn't contact anyone. Couldn't do anything a living person might. But it wasn't for long — that's what Borya had promised.

He wasn't even allowed to go online. Nor phone his friends and family. Because he was supposed to be dead and dead people couldn't go online. Or even use the phone.

Being dead really is boring, he thought as he looked out at the woodland that backed onto the house. The thick new leaves sparkled in the bright afternoon sun. He couldn't even go for a walk outside. Minty crossed the room and collapsed into the sofa. *It's just the doing nothing,* he thought, drumming an erratic percussive pattern on his knees. He just couldn't do nothing. He needed to do *something*.

But what?

Looking around the room, he saw the large screen TV and expensive music system. Sure, he could put some music on, or even watch a film, but those things were at best a distraction. At worst? A danger. What if he didn't hear the early warning system he'd installed on the front door? Resting his head in his hands, Minty rubbed his temples.

But it wasn't his safety that troubled him. Sure, being on edge was bad. But it was the thoughts of his family that haunted him the most.

A car engine groaned from the street outside. Minty held his breath until it faded back into the din of the city.

Letting his eyes close, he pictured them; his brother, mum and dad, expressions of grief etched into their eyes. He hoped they wouldn't blame each other.

He longed to contact them and tell them he was alive and well. He needed to explain the reasons behind why he was doing this. He had to speak to them soon because right now they thought he was dead.

29

Borya felt the sweet tang of the vodka slip down his throat. It tasted good.

The boss wanted him to head up some of the operations. This was a big move. He was going to be in charge.

"I've always known you had this in you," Olezka said, refilling their glasses. "For a long time now I've been thinking of my own retirement. Stepping away at least. Get a house on the coast maybe. No more of this running and chasing." He made a gesture of running fingers with his right hand before picking up the glass. "I just needed someone to step up for me. Someone with the right attributes. Na Zdorovie!" Olezka lifted the glass to his lips and drained it.

"Now, I have business to attend to. But before I do, I must pee."

"You know the way Dedushka Olezka," Borya said, draining his glass too.

Olezka left the room and Borya considered what they

had just discussed. He would be in charge. His years of hard work would have paid off.

Olezka's phone pinged from the countertop. Borya looked at it. A text message had been received. 'Semion' flashed on the screen.

Borya was alert. Had Semion got something from Keal? Borya reached over, spun the phone around and viewed the message. Reading the three words, Borya felt the room move. The air left his lungs and he gripped the counter for support.

"Borya was there," the text message said.

30

"Oh my gosh. Allissa. Hi! How are you?" Allissa's sister squealed. Allissa smiled, swallowing her nerves. "You look, just... wow," Lucy said, looking Allissa up and down. Allissa felt suddenly exposed in the clinging black dress.

"Archie, Mum, it's Allissa," Lucy shouted back into the house. "Well, you can't just stand out there," Lucy said and pulled Allissa into a hug, "come in, come in."

The hallway was just as Allissa remembered. Dark paintings hung across white walls. In the largest, a man pulled a reluctant horse through an orchard, but the horse seemed more interested in the apples than following its master. When Allissa lived in the house, she used to think that if it were her horse, she would either let it eat the apples or take it another route. It seemed unnecessarily cruel to be pulling it past fruit it wasn't allowed to eat. In contrast to the gloomy painting, a bright string of bunting drooped across the frame.

Lucy led them through the door Allissa had cowered behind the last time she was in the house.

"Oh, Allissa, it's so good to see you. You really must tell us everything," exclaimed Lucy as they waited in the kitchen for the hired butler to pour champagne. It was fair to say Lucy had put on weight since Allissa had last seen her. She now looked more like their father, which Allissa didn't think was a compliment.

"Yes, well, I don't know where to start," Allissa said. "It feels like so much has happened. It was so nice to get the invite though, thank you."

Smiling, Allissa looked around the kitchen. It had always been one of her favourite places in the house. Most of the other rooms felt far too formal, but here in the kitchen, with its thick oak counters, rustic dining table and its giant stove — which seemed to groan and tick all the time — Allissa felt comfortable. It was a place the pressures of the outside world didn't seem to permeate. They could just be a family here. That was until the day she'd heard the secret that had forced her to run.

"I just couldn't have you miss it," Lucy said, taking the glass the butler offered without acknowledgement.

"Thank you," Allissa said as she accepted hers.

"Especially because we're celebrating two things today," Lucy said.

"Oh, your birthday, and —"

Lucy waggled her podgy left hand in front of Allissa's face. A diamond ring gleamed from her fourth finger.

"Oh my gosh. Wow. I didn't even know you were... well, I just had no idea..."

"No, it was all a bit of a surprise. This morning. We were just having breakfast and he —"

"We are celebrating then," Allissa said, raising the glass.

"Yes, yes, yes! I'm so happy you're here!"

If Allissa thought Lucy was over-the-top pleased to see

her, then meeting her stepmother for the first time since her dad's trial was the opposite. Eveline had always been a fierce woman. A few years younger than her husband, Allissa thought Eveline must now be on the cusp of sixty. The last few years had not been kind to her. She had the pale, marble-like complexion of the Venus de Milo, just without the youthful, timeless innocence.

As Allissa followed Lucy into the orangery, Eveline watched her from across the salted rim of a Martini glass. Around the orangery — Allissa could never understand why it wasn't called a conservatory — twenty or so guests lounged and chatted.

Meeting with Eveline again was always going to be the trickiest. Allissa had planned to be at best friendly, and at worst civil. Allissa smiled as their eyes met. Eveline returned Allissa's smile with a look that even the room's buoyant atmosphere couldn't soften.

"Hi Eveline, hi," Allissa said, smiling harder as she followed Lucy across the room.

"Mummy, it's so great to see Allissa, isn't it? It's like, you know, we're,"— she indicated their brother Archie, who was engrossed in conversation with two blonde-haired women —"all back together again. It's almost like we're a fa —"

"Good to see you," Eveline said, pushing Allissa's outstretched hand to the side and pulling her into a rigid hug. Air kisses flew like bullets. "It's so nice of you to come."

Once again, Allissa got the impression she was merely Eveline's husband's daughter.

"Let's look at you then," Eveline said, holding Allissa at arm's length. "Yes, you look well. Have you been eating properly?"

"Yes, I —"

"I wouldn't want you to be going hungry or anything. Lovely dress. Who's it by?"

"I'm not sure. I bought it online."

"Oh, I see, well, very nice." Eveline considered Allissa through unblinking eyes. Around them, the babble and chatter of the party seemed to mute.

"It's nice of you to invite me," Allissa said after a thirsty sip of her champagne.

"Well, I... it's important we're all here. For Lucy. Excuse me," Eveline said, finishing two-thirds of her Martini in a single gulp. "I must go and get this refilled."

31

One of the worst things — well, not as bad as the thought of his family grieving his self-inflicted death, but still pretty bad — was the knowledge that everything was ready to go. Minty had been prepared to leave Berlin for weeks. The car, which he'd bought using cash from a man in Spandau, was packed and ready. Minty had chosen it especially to get them out of the city unnoticed; a cheap and inconspicuous ten-year-old VW Golf. Now, just like Minty himself, it was waiting.

He had even planned their destination. He'd actually planned a series of destinations. Each one was mapped out with highlighters in an old German road map he'd found on the bookshelf.

Minty glanced up at the bookshelf. Whoever lived in the house was a fan of fiction. Rows of dusty German paperbacks boasted the excitement of their contents with bright covers and snappy titles. Minty spoke German well and enjoyed reading, but right now he couldn't concentrate long enough for anything like that.

With a surge of sadness, Minty thought of his family. He

was supposed to have been able to tell them by now. He longed to let them know it was all fake, a trick designed to set him up for life.

But, right now, they thought he was dead. He registered the thought like a punch in the chest. He needed to tell them he was alright. He just needed to explain that he was alive and well and free. And share the exciting news behind why he had done this. But he couldn't. Not yet. He had to wait for a Russian. A Russian with half a million euros.

32

The sound of the toilet flushing drew Borya back into the present. Semion had found out. Semion knew that he had been in the shop with Minty.

This information changed things. Olezka would want to know why. Borya knew that Olezka wouldn't accept a simple answer. There was no logical reason for him to be at the shop. That wasn't his job.

Olezka knowing Borya had been at the shop would change things completely.

Borya shuddered as images of the decaying room and the spiralling blood filled his mind.

The sound of running water echoed from the bathroom. Borya imagined Olezka washing his hands. Soon he would head back this way. Borya needed to do something. He needed to do something now.

His eyes flicked from the phone to a block of glinting knives on the counter. Borya didn't think he had ever used the knives. He ate in restaurants every night. They would be sharp.

He slid one from the block. The smallest. Its metal

handle was cold to the touch. The blade glimmered hungrily.

He could kill Olezka right here in his apartment. Although Borya was smaller, Olezka wouldn't be armed. But then what? What would he do with the body? Olezka was a big man, much taller and heavier than Borya. Removing the body from the apartment on his own would be almost impossible without being seen. And what if the others found out?

No, he couldn't kill Olezka here. Maybe somewhere else, where he wouldn't have to move the body, but not here.

The tap in the bathroom shut off. Borya heard Olezka unlock the door. Then Olezka paused. Maybe he was looking at himself in the mirror.

No, he couldn't kill Olezka now. That left only one option. Borya glanced at the phone again.

Snatching the phone from the counter, Borya deleted the message.

"I'm glad we have had that discussion," Olezka said as he walked back into the room.

Borya slid the phone back down onto the counter, face down.

"I will start making arrangements in the next few days. Then we will meet and talk about the specifics."

Olezka glanced at his phone on the counter. His eyes momentarily narrowed, and his finger extended towards it.

"It would be my honour, Dedushka Olezka," Borya said, smiling.

"Yes," Olezka said, picking up the phone and stashing it back inside his coat. "You will be great for this city."

Olezka placed his powerful arms on Borya's slender shoulders. Borya felt himself strain against the weight.

"You will be great for this city," Olezka repeated. "Now

rest today. There is a lot of work coming for you and I need you in good form."

"Thank you," Borya said, following the older man to the door. Although Borya smiled, inside he twisted and writhed.

He needed to go. He needed to go now.

33

Back in his hotel room, Leo took the grimy phone from his pocket. As expected, it wasn't turning on. The battery was flat, or the phone was damaged beyond use. It had been in a collision with a train after all. Leo turned it around in his hands. The screen was a spider's web of cracks, and the back casing was split.

Leo rummaged through his bag for a charging cable. He hoped it would just be a flat battery as that was easy to fix. Fortunately, Leo's phone used the same charger. Leo forced the charging cable into the European adapter and plugged it all in.

Then, holding his breath, he looked at the screen. Nothing happened. He wiggled the plug. Still, nothing happened. He tried turning the adapter and fitting it in the other way around. Nothing.

With a grumble of frustration, Leo slumped to the bed. Maybe it was just broken. It had been in a collision with a train. If that was the case, then there was nothing Leo could do. There was no way he would even know it was Minty's.

But wait...

Something on the screen of the phone had changed...

Leo squinted and leaned in. There was something there. Beneath the web of cracks, he could just about make out the ghostly image of the charging symbol. It was as though the light that illuminated the screen had died, but the display was still showing.

Leo picked up the phone to get a better look. The charging symbol disappeared.

Bugger.

He must have upset the delicate cable assembly. He replaced the phone exactly where it was, and sure enough, a few seconds later the spectral image of a jagged lightning bolt reappeared.

Leo waited a full five minutes before he risked touching the phone again. Then, holding down the power button, he watched as the faint charging symbol faded and in its place, a ghostly logo appeared. A few seconds later, the logo disappeared and Leo was asked for a passcode.

The passcode. Damn.

There would be a workaround to cracking it, but that would take time. Leo sent a message to Charles Rolleston asking for any suggestions.

Charles replied two minutes later with four possibilities.

Leo carefully entered the first one. The phone thought about it for a second.

Incorrect passcode.

The second and third had the same response.

The final one was a six-digit code. Looking closely to make sure he got the right keys on the broken screen, Leo typed it in. Then pressed enter. The screen went dark.

Then, from the darkness, a few ghostly icons appeared.

Careful not to dislodge the cable, Leo started scrolling through some of the menus and apps. It was hard to see anything on the dark screen, but at a particular angle light from the window exposed the faint image.

First, Leo looked at the sent messages. Nothing; both received and sent boxes were empty. Then he scrolled to the pictures. Again, empty. But one call had been made from the phone. Leo cross-checked it with his phone; it was Charles' number.

Leo once again got the feeling that something wasn't right. Something didn't stack up. Straightening up, he flexed his shoulders. A knot was appearing at the top of his back. Rubbing between his shoulder blades, he glanced at his phone on the bed. He didn't care about phones, yet he owned a newer model than this. There had been two or three new models since this one actually. Having been through Minty's social media accounts, Leo knew he did a lot of his business on the internet. He was always posting about the new designs he was working on or where he was travelling. It felt unlikely that a well-connected, sociable and wealthy man would use a five-year-old phone. Of course, it was possible but unlikely.

An instinct thronged through Leo's veins.

Leo snatched his phone from the duvet and called the one person he needed to talk to right now. The one person he relied on more than his instincts.

34

Olezka pulled the Rolls Royce to a stop outside the abandoned bakery and killed the engine. He stood from the car and stretched. The morning had been a productive one. He had caught a thief and worked out who was going to help him in the next iteration of his organisation.

It was important they moved with the times and for that, Olezka knew, he needed to get some young blood in the driving seat. Berlin was changing, and so his organisation had to change too. That was the way the world worked.

Olezka pulled open the door and stepped into the old building. The screams that had reverberated from the bare walls were silent. That problem had been dealt with.

"Dedushka Olezka," Semion said as Olezka stepped into the room.

Keal was still tied to the chair with his head lolling forwards. Olezka couldn't tell if he was dead or alive, and didn't care either way.

"Did you get my message?" Semion asked. "I didn't

believe it myself at first, so I had him say it again. I have it recorded for you."

Semion pointed at the camera and tripod in front of Keal's wilted figure. Semion was looking through the footage on a laptop.

"I can show you now if you like. As I say, I had him say it again, just to make sure. With these drugs the person speaks without being conscious of it, so it cannot be a lie. I'll call it up now." Semion tapped ferociously on the computer.

"Semion," Olezka said, holding up a hand, "what are you talking about?"

Semion turned and considered the boss with pale eyes. "Did you get the message?"

Olezka shook his head and pulled out his phone. "No, no messages," he said.

"I definitely —"

"What did it say?"

Semion tapped at the laptop again and a video began to play. Olezka stepped closer. Keal writhed on the screen and Semion's recorded voice sounded from the speakers.

"Borya was there," came Keal's reply.

Olezka's phone clattered to the floor and Semion stopped the video.

"No, carry on, don't stop it you idiot." Olezka waved at the computer. Semion started it again and Olezka stared in disbelief.

Keal's words echoed from the laptop. When he had finished, Semion stopped the video.

"Keal always picked up the same number of parcels as he brought to you," Semion said. "I've checked the last ten visits against your records."

Olezka's jaw opened and then snapped shut. A dark

expression shadowed his face as he looked at Keal's crumpled body.

"What car did he say he saw outside?" Olezka asked.

Semion checked his notes. "A red Maserati."

Olezka nodded. "Interesting." Olezka tapped the bulge of his gun beneath his jacket. "Borya has been stealing. The little snake." Olezka crossed the room and placed his hand on Keal's neck. The man's pulse was faint and erratic. "With all I've done for him."

Olezka pulled out his pistol. He sank to his knees and looked into Keal's vacant eyes.

"I'm sorry *rebenok*. Borya will pay for this."

Olezka stood up and levelled the gun at Keal's head. A single shot echoed through the derelict building.

"Semion, pack up here," Olezka said, heading for the door. "I need to speak to someone about a Maserati, and then we'll go and pay Borya a visit."

35

Leo dropped his phone to the bed. Allissa must be at the party. That was good; he wanted her to enjoy herself. She hadn't seen her family in years and although she'd never admitted it, Leo knew that she missed them.

Leo walked to the window and looked out at the three identical buildings around the small plaza. A few bedraggled plants struggled out of large pots, and two large bins overflowed. In one corner, three small children bounced and caught a ball. Leo guessed they were from somewhere in the Middle East. A woman in a blue hijab appeared at the door of one of the ground floor apartments and waved her flour-covered forearms at the children. Perhaps dinner was ready. The largest child caught the ball, and they ran together, skirting a pile of broken glass and skipping over a rusted bike with one wheel.

Leo smiled. He didn't know the family, but they seemed happy and safe. Leo had read multiple stories of people from warring Middle Eastern countries settling all over Europe and wondered if that was their story. It was interesting how people came to Berlin for all sorts of reasons; some for the fashion, some for the clubs and bars, others for something more fundamental — like safety.

Leo's lips pursed in thought. Minty had enjoyed the clubs of Berlin. Charles had been over a few times and they'd been clubbing together. He'd said it was like nowhere else he'd ever been.

Minty was killed at 4 am.

Leo rubbed his chin in thought, then his expression dissolved completely.

Why had he not thought of this before?

How had he not made this connection?

There was no reason for a fashion designer to be up at 4 am unless he was on his way back from a club.

With both Minty's shop and the flat within ten minutes' walk of the station, Leo assumed he'd gone straight to the station from either one of those. But the fact Minty may have been going home changed things. Something could have happened at the club, or he could have met someone there.

Leo opened a map of Berlin on his phone. With a few taps, he populated it with the city's nightclubs. There must have been over fifty scattered across central Berlin. That was far too many to be working with.

Why would a city need so many nightclubs anyway? Weren't they all pretty much the same?

Zooming in, Leo looked at those near the U-Bahn station. That didn't mean anything, though — two lines connected at Kottbusser Tor station. Minty could have arrived on a train from almost anywhere in the city.

Leo looked at Minty's phone and was struck by a thought. With someone's phone, you could see where they'd been. Smartphones recorded their location, which was why people with dishonest intentions often used low tech "burner" phones.

Plugging Minty's phone into his laptop, Leo entered the passcode again and launched the 'Find your Phone' app. A map of Berlin filled the screen. If Minty had been using the phone for long, the map would be scrawled with his routes and destinations. The phone had only recorded two.

At first, the two recorded locations showed up as coordinates. Then, as the hotel's creaky Wi-Fi caught up, they changed to place names and addresses.

The first one was the U-Bahn station, and the second, as Leo had expected, was a nightclub.

36

Borya thumbed the entry bell then stood back from the door. As his breath rattled in his chest, he resisted the urge to double over. The walk from his apartment in Kreuzberg to Prenzlauer Berg had taken an hour. He would normally take the car, but he couldn't risk anyone seeing that. As for a taxi or public transport — that was out of the question too. Olezka knew people everywhere — that was the problem. A walk through the backstreets was always going to be safer. At least that way he could watch closely for anyone following him.

Anafisa's Maserati Laventi rested at the kerb, which meant she was definitely at home. Borya had known Anafisa since she'd moved to Berlin about two years ago. She too was Russian but had moved to the city looking for a fresh start after the death of her husband. Borya didn't think she'd seemed very upset about becoming widowed unless spending his money was part of the grieving process.

"Come on," he muttered, knitting his fingers together.

He was just about to press the button again when Anafisa's sultry voice oozed from the speaker.

"Hallo."

Borya knew he didn't have many options. Almost everyone he knew was loyal to Olezka, so would now be looking for him. Anafisa was the only person, as far as he knew, who wasn't.

"Anafisa, let me in," Borya hissed breathlessly. "Something's happened. I need to come in."

The speaker clunked and Borya heard a faint voice.

"Sure sure," Anafisa said. "I'll let you up."

The door buzzed and Borya headed inside. Anafisa's penthouse was in one of Berlin's most expensive neighbourhoods. Her apartment occupied the whole top floor and the roof terrace, complete with hot tub, had views of the city skyline.

Borya took the marble stairs two at a time. On the third floor, he passed a young man coming down. He had the look of someone who had just been woken up. His hair was spiked at the back and he was still pulling on a jumper.

Anafisa was in the kitchen rinsing a pair of wine glasses as Borya walked in. As ever, she looked glamorous.

"Anafisa, I need your help," Borya said.

"What is it?" she replied, looking up.

Although Anafisa must have been well into her forties, she looked about thirty. Her porcelain skin was supple, and her sensuous lips were coloured a deep red. As Borya crossed the kitchen, she smiled, revealing a triangle of glimmering white teeth.

Anafisa was, Borya had thought many times, a beautiful woman.

"Sit down." Anafisa directed Borya to the sofa in the corner. "I'll bring us some drinks."

"I need to get out of Berlin, now," Borya said.

Anafisa walked towards him with two glasses of wine.

Borya slurped greedily from the wine and told Anafisa what had happened. She listened, her wide eyes watching him closely.

"Could you just put Olezka out of his misery? He's old now anyway. It'll save someone else doing it later."

"How would I do that? I couldn't get within a hundred metres of him."

"Poison him or something," Anafisa said. "It'll be fun." Anafisa took a sip of the wine and a dribble of it ran from the corner of her plump lips. Her eyes glowed mischievously.

"No," Borya said. "It's not possible."

"No fun. Do you have the packages?" Anafisa asked.

"Not yet, Minty… urrrr… someone else has them. I need to get them from him and sell them, then we're splitting the money. I expected to have more time than this."

Anafisa nodded. "How quickly can you do that?"

"I'm supposed to be collecting them from Minty tonight. But now Olezka knows, maybe I should just leave it. I'll get out of the city. It's not safe for me here."

"You should continue with your deal," Anafisa said. "Get the money and I'll get you out of the city for a few months. Things are changing around here soon anyway. I have a place in the Alps. It was my husband's, God rest him. He liked skiing there."

"Could you do that?" Borya asked.

"Of course," Anafisa said, kissing Borya. "We'll get you a car and you can go in a couple of days."

Borya took a sip of the wine and felt his mood improving. A few months away from the city with half a million euros. He could do that.

"You need to relax. Go and run yourself a bath," Anafisa

said, slipping Borya's coat from his shoulders. "I'll join you in a minute."

Borya smiled. He knew what that meant.

Anafisa listened as Borya walked into the bathroom. When she heard the bath running, she stepped out onto the roof terrace and punched a number into her phone.

"He's here as you said he would be."

"Yes."

"This will be my debt paid, yes?"

"I'll keep you informed."

37

"When I first met Lu Lu," said Lucy's fiancé Jasper, addressing the party, "I just knew there was something special about her."

Lucy wrinkled her nose at the compliment.

Allissa watched the scene the way a scientist might scrutinize the contents of a petri dish.

"When we first spoke, that evening at the Commodore Club, I'd just... I'd just never seen someone quite so... delectable."

Lucy giggled and turned to scan the room.

Allissa drained her third gin and tonic and slid the empty glass onto the table. With fondness she thought of the dark backstreet pubs Leo and herself frequented the world over. She would take some dingy boozer over this pomp and pageantry any day. Pinning a smile to her face, she wondered what her life would have been like if she'd stayed living in the Stockwell family home. Just one of the sofas here, upholstered in fabric made by monks in the Andes —or some shit like that — would probably cost more than all the furniture in Leo and Allissa's flat combined.

Allissa watched Jasper wax lyrical about his future wife and wondered if she would have ended up married to a man like him too. The more Jasper spoke, the more Allissa found the thought — and the man — repugnant.

"It was really at my parents' place in Tuscany though, that I decided Lucy was the woman for me. We were..."

As Jasper gesticulated with his glass, Allissa thought of the champagne she'd shared with the girls the night they'd finally opened the guesthouse in Kathmandu. She remembered the genuine laughter which had echoed through the building that night. A million miles from the polite and incoherent tittering around her tonight.

Given a choice, Allissa would much rather be on the sofa with Leo.

With that thought of Leo, Allissa felt the need to check her phone. He hadn't been in touch all afternoon. He'd been in Berlin for hours now so he must have something to tell her. He was supposed to keep her in the loop. That was the deal.

As though answering her thoughts, Allissa felt her bag vibrate. Flipping the lid, she looked inside. Her phone glowed with an incoming call from Leo.

"And then when I met the family," Jasper droned, "Eveline, Archie and Blake. You all made me so welcome..."

Allissa scanned the room. Could she slip out and get this?

"Such a shame Blake can't be with us today. We really hope the powers that be see some sense when the appeal goes to court."

Allissa looked up from the phone at the assembled people, all listening to Jasper.

"I know Lucy would love so much for her father to walk her down the aisle..."

Every pair of eyes were fixed on the man giving the speech — every pair of eyes but one. Allissa felt Eveline's pale gaze boring into her.

Allissa clenched her teeth, smiled and slid the phone back into her bag. She couldn't leave now. She'd have to talk to Leo later.

38

Looking at himself in the mirror, Minty groaned. He used to take so much pride in his appearance — appearance used to be everything — but right now, his reflection was nothing but a disappointment.

Grey and ashen, he looked as though the apprehension of his situation was draining the life from him. His eyes, which used to be bright and engaging, were now red and sunken. He rubbed a hand across his face and blinked hard. It would all be over soon. It would have to be.

Even his hair, which used to shine, now hung bleak and lifeless. *Maybe there's some rough justice in this,* he thought, turning the black beanie hat in his fingers. The thing that he'd always been proud of — the way he looked — was being taken from him.

It'll be over soon though, he thought again as he pulled the black hat down over his matted hair.

Minty was going to meet the Russian. It wasn't safe to use the phone, apparently, so they had arranged to meet somewhere.

Minty longed to be able to use his phone again. Just to

call his family and tell them he was alive and well. Even getting a message to them would be enough, just so long as their suffering was over.

Pulling a black jacket from the back of a chair, Minty promised himself that when this was all over, he'd never lose touch with his family again. He zipped the jacket and stepped back to look at his reflection in the mirror. Gone were the colours he used to love wearing. Now he wore only black, for fear of standing out. That wouldn't be for long, he thought. As soon as this was over, he would be the loudest person in the room again. With the hint of a smile, Minty pulled a bright yellow scarf from his bag. This would be the first thing he wore to celebrate his coming freedom. Walking to the front door, Minty hung the scarf over the handle. When this was all over, he'd leave this house with the scarf around his shoulders. With that thought came a small wave of contentment.

Minty turned to face the window. The sun had begun its descent behind the woodland. When darkness had fallen, he would head out. Tonight the Russian should have his money. Maybe in a few hours he would be wearing the yellow scarf on his way out of the city. Minty hoped so.

39

"It's got to be here somewhere," Olezka said.

Semion prized the door of Borya's apartment open. The lock splintered and shards of wood scattered across the floor.

Olezka knew Borya wouldn't be there. Borya was smarter than that. But he may not have had a chance to move the stuff yet.

"Look everywhere," Olezka said, pulling out one of the kitchen drawers. Cutlery crashed to the floor. "I'll start in here. You start in the bedroom. Look for the packages or money."

It's a long shot, he thought, tearing open one of the cupboards and throwing the plates onto the floor. But they needed to be sure.

In the bedroom, Semion rifled through drawers and wardrobes. The guy didn't have much stuff. He flipped the mattress, looked under the bed, pulled the pictures from the wall and ripped the side from the bath. Nothing. The place was empty.

Ten minutes later, the two men met in the living room. The place was ransacked.

"Nothing here Dedushka Olezka," Semion said. "But he left in a hurry. He's not packed or anything."

The shrill ring of Olezka's phone pierced the silence of the room.

"Da," he said, holding the phone to his ear. "I see." A grin spread across his face. "Yes, keep me informed."

40

Epitome Nightclub was a shambolic collection of buildings in Berlin's Rummelsburg district. Leo checked the map on his phone to make sure that the decaying structure really was an operational nightclub. Even in the coming darkness the place looked rundown.

Leo had checked the venue's website before leaving the hotel, although the place didn't open until midnight, he guessed someone must be around to set up for the event. Leo walked towards what he assumed must be the main entrance and knocked as hard as he could. There was no reply.

The website boasted that one of Europe's leading techno groups was playing tonight. A pair of DJs called The Space Camels. Unsurprisingly, Leo had never heard of them.

Leo knocked on the door again. Still no reply.

Leo looked around the yard, graffiti covered most of the walls and crates of empty bottles were stacked in one corner. In a few hours, techno music would be thudding from these walls as people queued to get in. Leo felt a strange tinge of excitement at the prospect.

Although he frequently enjoyed a few beers, it was several years since Leo'd been clubbing. At university, he'd grown bored of the clubs playing cheesy music to predatory drunk people. Here, even on the outside, it all seemed different.

A door to the side of the building clattered open and a man rushed into the yard carrying three crates of empty bottles.

"Hey," Leo shouted, "excuse me? Hello!"

The guy turned, then in a moment of imbalance, dropped one of the crates. It crashed to the floor. Bottles skittered and smashed.

"Ah, fuck!" the guy shouted.

"I'm so sorry, I didn't mean to..." Leo said, running across the yard to help.

"What are you doing here?" the man replied.

Leo was surprised to hear a Californian accent.

"I'm.. I'm... looking for help with something," Leo said, picking up two unbroken bottles and slotting them back into a crate. "My brother..." Leo had decided to pretend Minty was his brother. "Fell beneath a U-Bahn train last week. This club was the last place he visited. I'm wondering if there would be any CCTV footage of him here."

"I'll be back in a minute," the guy said. He went back inside the nightclub and returned with a dustpan and brush. "I've got so much to do tonight as well. Just what I need."

Leo picked up the dustpan and tipped the shards in the bin.

"You say this was the last place he visited?"

"Yeah, I've just recovered his phone, and this was the last location he visited —"

"What, you can do that?"

"Yeah, it's pretty simple. He left just before 4 am."

"When was this?" The yard was now almost dark.

"Last Sunday morning."

"Ahh, we had the Luuka Syence on until 6 am. Busy night. Open until 10 am."

"I just want to get any information about that night. Do you have CCTV in the club?" Leo asked.

"You know, if we were in California there'd be a camera on every wall, but not Berlin. Clubbing's a private thing here, you know? What happens in there" — he pointed towards the building — "stays in there."

Leo's curiosity piqued.

"There's one camera above the door there," the guy said, pointing up at it. "And one on the far wall there. Gets a picture of people as they enter and leave. Helps us if there's ever any trouble with people not being allowed in."

"But nothing else?"

"Nope. There's even a *no phones* policy. I mean, people still do, but it's not allowed."

"Do you think I'd be able to see that CCTV footage? I want to see if he came with anyone —"

"I... I'm not sure..." The guy looked at his watch. "Shit. I'm late. Totally up against it tonight. Three of my bar people just called in sick. What about if you come back —"

"I'll help you," Leo said.

"What?"

"If you let me look through these CCTV images now, I'll help you set up for your event tonight."

The guy narrowed his eyes. "You ever worked a bar before?"

"Sure, loads of times in England." Leo lied.

"Alright," he said, stepping forward with an outstretched hand. "I'm Lance. Good to meet you." Leo introduced himself.

"Help me set up and then we'll have a look through the CCTV. If you stay for the shift, I'll pay ya. You'll not work for nothing."

"Deal," Leo said, shaking Lance by the hand.

Lance explained what Leo needed to know as they walked through the dark nightclub.

"This is room one," he said. Angular speakers hung from the ceiling and lights bristled from the corners. "This is where the Space Camels will be playing later. Proper techno. You been to Berlin before?"

Leo shook his head.

"Then you've never heard anything like it. Make sure you get in here and have a listen. It'll change your life. Out here's the main bar. We'll sort this one out and get one of the others to do the rest —"

"How many bars are there?"

"Three in total, but this one's the biggest. I'll have you with me here so I can help if needed. First, we need to get these empties taken out, then stock the fridges."

The next two hours flew by as Leo and Lance shifted crates of empty bottles, filled the fridges and replenished the spirits. When they'd finished Lance poured them both a beer.

"Another good thing about this place," Lance said, handing Leo the glass, "drinking on the job is pretty much encouraged. I'm not sure I could do it without it."

"Yeah, you must have seen some sights," Leo said.

"Totally. Right, let's have a look at this CCTV. Bring your beer."

Following Lance through the club, Leo looked into the two smaller rooms where different DJs would play later that evening. Lance stopped by a curtain and turned to Leo.

"This is something I've never seen anywhere but in

Berlin

Berlin. Every club here has one." Lance pulled aside the curtain and Leo peered in. Two sofas faced each other at either end of a small space which, when the curtain was dropped, would be in complete darkness.

"What do people use it for?" Leo asked, instantly feeling stupid for his innocence.

"I know what I would use it for." Lance grinned. "You wait until you see some of the women."

Lance flicked a knowing nod to Leo, all Leo could think about was Allissa in the figure-hugging dress.

At the end of a passageway, Lance unlocked a door. Leo followed him inside.

In the centre of the room, a table was strewn with documents. The walls were covered with posters from previous events.

"It's never as glamourous as you'd think," Lance said as Leo looked around the office. Lance sat at the desk and lifted the screen of a laptop. "You know, in films, where someone goes to see the nightclub boss, and he's got that real swanky office. It's never like that in reality."

"Yeah, really disappointing," Leo said. "I bet you don't even pull people's fingernails off in here either."

"Afraid not. Fill in loads of spreadsheets though."

Lance logged into the computer and the CCTV system's control panel appeared.

"All these CCTV systems are cloud-based now. It's a lot easier than it used to be. What dates and times are we looking for?"

Leo gave Lance the date and time he expected Minty to have left the club.

"I'll go to ten minutes before then we'll run through it at speed. You tell me if you see him."

Leo scrutinized the people on the screens shuffling to and from the club. It must have been a busy night.

"What's that," Leo said, noticing a man walk from a different direction as everyone else.

"That's a fire escape. We use it for staff to come and go during the night and the DJs are brought in that way. Customers shouldn't be using it, though. Is that him?"

Leo squinted at the image. It was a small man, pale-skinned and with what looked like a long thick coat hanging from his shoulders.

"No, it's not. It just looked unusual. Carry on."

As the man in the green coat wandered away, another man appeared.

"Pause again," Leo said, scrutinising the height, size and hair colour. "That's him, I think. I'm sure of it. Just hold there for a second."

Unlocking his phone, Leo noticed it had been on silent and he'd missed a call from Allissa. He cancelled the notification, brought up the camera and took a picture.

"Can you scroll back? I want to get a picture of that other guy too."

Lance scrolled the video back and Leo took another photo.

At that moment a thunderous bass rumbled through the walls of the building. It shot through Leo's spine. In a panic, he looked around the office.

"Don't worry," Lance shouted, putting a hand on Leo's shoulder, "that's just the guys making sure the sound system's working properly. The main dancefloor is just through this wall."

Leo took a deep breath to calm himself.

"This definitely isn't like the movies," Leo shouted above the noise.

41

"Why did you choose to meet him here?" Anafisa asked, swinging the Maserati Levante from the main road and into the suburban district of Charlottenburg.

Borya liked being a passenger in the Maserati. Lots of people *drove* cars, but Anafisa *mastered* the car. She moved through the gears with such speed that Borya was pinned to the seat.

Maybe when I have my Rolls Royce, Borya thought, *I'll get Anafisa to drive me around in it.*

"It just seemed like a good place. In the middle of nowhere. No one would think of it, right?" Borya removed the pipe from his lips and exhaled. A thick cloud of smoke streamed out the window.

"It's a Cold War spy station," Anafisa said. "Could you get any more dramatic?"

Borya grinned. "It's a good place. I think it's the perfect place. There's no way Olezka will be coming all the way out here. No way."

The road straightened out and Anafisa glanced at Borya.

"I just hope Minty's got the stuff tonight," Borya said.

"Why wouldn't he?"

"Because I haven't got the money for him. I was supposed to get him his half of the money and then pay him so that he could get out of the city. He doesn't want to hang around. Thinks the more he hangs around, the more likely his cover will get blown."

"How much were you supposed to take?" Anafisa asked, acting casual.

"Half a million euros."

Anafisa pursed her lips.

"He is in no danger," Borya continued. "His cover's good. I arranged it myself. It'll be fine for another day anyway."

Anafisa pouted and slowed for a tight corner. "So, you're going to sell the stuff and then bring him the money tomorrow?"

Borya nodded.

"Why will he trust you to do that?"

Borya looked at Anafisa as he felt the car accelerate out of a corner. "He'll have to trust me. It'll be a leap of faith."

Above them on the hill, the domes of Teufelsberg loomed. The Maserati was streaming past thick trees on both sides of the road and somewhere in the distance the red outline of the city glowed.

As the Maserati's thick tyres screeched around another corner, Anafisa glanced at Borya. Her lips became a grim line as one thought circulated her mind: *tomorrow night Borya will be coming back up here with half a million euros.*

42

Minty felt himself shiver as he stepped into the woodland's impenetrable darkness. Behind him, the houses of Charlottenberg glimmered. The only house in darkness was the one in which he was staying. The place was supposed to be empty. The 'For Sale' sign and the drawn curtains added to the impression. Minty knew that one glimpse by a curious observer could ruin it all, as could someone seeing him walking into the woodland in the middle of the night. The people after him were well connected.

Seriously? Minty thought as he gripped the stem of his torch. The people living next to him were just normal people. They were a family, living in an expensive district of the city. Not gangster informants.

Minty cursed himself as he turned back to face the darkened path. It was ridiculous. It was all ridiculous. He'd spent far too long listening to the Russian's suspicions.

Minty exhaled. The mist of his breath curled in the cold night air. As with a lot of things the Russian did, there was some strange artistry about meeting up here. Poetry that in different circumstances, Minty would have found amusing.

With Berlin far beyond the Iron Curtain, the place was built by the Americans to eavesdrop into what was going on around them. There was no knowing what secrets had been intercepted and decoded here. Now though, like much of Berlin's history, it lay in ruins. A playground for graffiti artists, squatters and the occasional tourist looking for something different.

Tonight, though, the thick concrete walls would only ring with the whispers shared by Borya and himself.

Twenty minutes later, Minty looked out at the city simmering a few miles to the east. The Berliner Fernsehturm — *the Television Tower* — scratched the sky with its strobing point. The listening station's structure was taller than the surrounding woodland. Its sides were unprotected from the elements. Tatters of some kind of cover skipped in the breeze. Minty shivered as a cold wind pushed from the west.

"You better have some good news for me," Minty said as Borya stepped out from the stairwell. He recognised the man from his outline against the luminous city. The long coat thrashed in the cutting wind.

"Hey, my man," Borya said, stretching out a hand. "Of course, I am always here for news. Borya does not come all the way up here when there is much business to do just for a, how you say? A chit chat?"

"Well?" Minty scowled. "You have my money?"

"There has been a slight problem. I don't have the money yet. Things have got a little bit difficult."

"What?"

"Well my plan has been discovered, so I have not been

able to get the money. But if you can give me the stuff now, I will sell it and bring you the money tomorrow."

"That was not the deal," Minty said. "You were bringing the money now, we were trading for the stuff and then you were going to sell it yourself.

"Yes, you're right. This is inconvenient. But you know, this is art." The Russian twisted his hand in the air flamboyantly.

"Borya, it's not art. It's not the deal we made."

"You know, that's the problem with you," the Russian said, turning to look back towards the city. "I bring you to the best view of the city. The best city in the world. My city —"

"I don't care about the view or your city. I care about my money,"— Minty felt his pulse quicken —"the money you are going to give me. I don't have time for your games. My family think I'm dead. These guys are already on to you and you want me to just sit around and do nothing."

Borya continued to stare at the city. Then he turned. "Yes, I see. I can understand why you are worried. That is a very troubling thing for your family to think. I am, of course, very sorry about it. But that's the way business goes sometimes. So, if you give me the shipments now, I'll take them, sell them tomorrow and then you'll have the money."

"How do I know I can trust you?"

"You have my word. I will be here in 24 hours with your money."

Minty looked out at the city brooding on the horizon. He knew he didn't really have a choice. If he wanted his money, he would have to play the Russian's game.

"Okay," Minty said.

"Good." Borya turned brightly. "I'll take the stuff then."

"That's the thing"— it was Minty's turn to smile — "you'll have to go and collect it."

43

"Quickly, get it open," Olezka said as Semion fumbled with the shutter of Minty's shop. They had found nothing in the apartment. Nothing. Borya had either taken it all with him — which Olezka doubted because he had to leave it in a hurry — or he'd already hidden it somewhere else. Olezka knew that often the simplest solutions were the best, so maybe the packages hadn't left the shop to begin with.

"Got it," Semion said as the shutter rattled upwards. He unlocked the door and the two men stepped inside. Olezka found the light switch and the overhead fluorescent bulbs flickered to life. The shop was exactly as Olezka had remembered. Clothes in an assortment of mad colours hung from a rail on the right-hand side. On the opposite wall, other garments were piled on shelves.

"Do people really buy this shit?" Semion said, pulling a shirt from the rail. It was made from some kind of shiny blue fabric. "Actually," he said as he held it up against himself, "I quite like —"

"We need to find those packages," Olezka bellowed.

"They've got to be in here somewhere. You look in here, and I'll take the back room."

———

"He left the packages in the shop the entire time?" Anafisa asked as they sped down the hill.

"Yeah, they're hidden in a secret compartment Minty found when he was renovating the place. He reckons it was some hiding place constructed during the war. Minty says there's no chance it'll be discovered."

"Clever guy," Anafisa said and nodded. She dabbed her foot on the brake and the Maserati slid around a corner. Dark woodland flashed past the windows. "Do you want to go there now?"

"Yeah, we might as well."

Anafisa toed the accelerator and they sped off towards the city.

44

Olezka knew there was a methodical skill to searching for things. But, unfortunately, that was a skill Olezka knew he didn't have. It was the same reason he wasn't good at interrogating. He was impatient. He just asked the questions he wanted the answers to. And if he didn't get them, he caused the person a lot of pain until they told him.

Olezka straightened up and looked around the small room. He had emptied every box, pulled open and tipped out every drawer, but there was no sign of the packages. Olezka sneered. He didn't like people getting the better of him, especially people who should have been loyal.

Olezka stepped back into the front of the shop and kicked a basket of cotton across the floor. Semion was searching methodically along the back wall. Olezka watched him removing a pile of clothes, feeling between them checking the wall behind, then returning the clothes to where they were. The parts he'd already searched looked unchanged from the rest. He had no idea how the man had the patience for that.

Olezka shook his head. That wasn't the way they did things either. Olezka would make sure they smashed the place up a bit before leaving.

ANAFISA KNEW the way to the shop so drove quickly without the need for directions. She had driven Borya there a couple of weeks ago. At the time she had no idea what it was for. Borya had said he needed to stop by as they had been passing.

Borya sat silently in the Maserati's passenger seat, smoking his pipe and watching the city roll past.

When they approached the shop, Borya stashed the pipe away and stared apprehensively through the windscreen. As the shop came into view, he exhaled sharply and pointed down the street.

"Bastards," he shouted. "Stop, stop!"

Anafisa applied the brake and the Maserati screamed to a halt.

"Look!" Borya shook an extended finger towards the windscreen. About halfway down the road, a dark car was parked up on the kerb.

"That's Olezka's Rolls Royce. They're looking for the packages now."

"Are you sure?" Anafisa looked from the Rolls Royce to Borya. "What do you want to do?"

Images of the abandoned bakery, the metal chair and the pooling blood ran through Borya's mind. "There's nothing we can do. We'll have to come back tomorrow."

"What if they find what they're looking for?"

"They won't," Borya said through a grin. "Unless they think to push the sink."

OLEZKA OPENED the door to the toilet cubicle and snapped on the light. They'd been searching for over an hour and had nothing to show for it. Olezka was frustrated.

The tiny toilet cubicle was the only place they hadn't torn apart. Every inch of both the shop and the back room had been checked several times for packages, hidden spaces and secret compartments. But they'd found nothing.

Olezka examined the room. The toilet cubicle was no bigger than a phone box. The grubby toilet had an old-fashioned cistern on the wall above it. There was a small sink on the left wall and a metal bucket full of cleaning products below. Olezka stepped into the tiny space. His elbows almost touched walls.

Olezka dropped the toilet seat, stood on it and tore the lid from the cistern. He pulled the chain and the water drained. There was nothing unusual in there. He stepped back down and his foot struck the bucket of cleaning products. Bottles of bleach and glass cleaner rolled across the floor.

Olezka swore under his breath and stepped backwards. He felt his hip push past the sink. Then he felt something move. Olezka was suddenly alert. He looked back into the cubicle. Had the sink really moved?

"Sinks don't move," Olezka whispered, "unless...?"

The shrill ringing of Olezka's phone filled the shop. He dragged it from his pocket and answered the call. It was Anafisa.

45

"Olezka," Anafisa said. She pulled the dressing gown tight around her shoulders against the cold night wind. The city below was quiet. Borya had already fallen asleep. Any man would after what they'd just done.

Olezka's voice grumbled down the line.

"I know where Borya will be with your money tomorrow," Anafisa said.

"Good, where?"

"I'm not going to tell you right now. Listen to me very closely."

Olezka swore and began to argue but Anafisa cut him off.

"I know he's going to have half a million euros with him. That's ten times what I owe you. So, I want a bigger cut."

"You'll get nothing if you —" Olezka raised his voice but Anafisa interrupted him.

"Olezka, you can shout all you want but let me make it really clear to you. I want one-hundred thousand. Plus my debt written off."

"Why would I do that? You must think I'm crazy."

"If you say no?" Anafisa laughed into the night air. "Then I'll kill Borya myself and take it all."

There was silence down the line as Olezka considered his options. Anafisa knew he didn't really have any.

"Good, I'm glad you've decided to agree with me. I'll call you tomorrow and tell you where we're going. Be ready."

Anafisa hung up the phone and looked across Berlin. Maybe it was time she also went somewhere else to live.

46

Borya stepped from Anafisa's apartment and into the bright, cloudless afternoon. He couldn't believe Minty had done this to him. Leaving the packages hidden in the shop was both stupid and, Borya had to admit, brilliant. Borya just hoped the hiding place was as good as Minty thought. Olezka and his men wouldn't have given up easily.

Borya ducked into a kiosk and grabbed a drink from the fridge.

"Danke, behalte das Wechselgeld." *Thanks, keep the change.*

Taking a deep swig of the Club Mate, a carbonated energy drink made from some kind of magic root, Borya waved to the group of men sat at the small table outside the kiosk. A growing pile of empty beer bottles and an orange cloud of cigarette smoke surrounded them.

As a man accustomed to driving everywhere, Borya thought it was nice to walk occasionally. Of course, his desire to make this trip on foot had nothing to do with exercise. It was much more important than that. In a vehicle, Borya thought he had a higher chance of being followed.

Taking another long sip of the Club Mate, Borya turned the corner onto Reichenberger Strasse. To his right, a steel pillar covered with posters showed upcoming events in the city. Borya didn't need to check boards like this to know the events. He had people who would do that for him.

Borya glanced in the darkened window of an apothecary as he passed to check no one was following him on foot. It was essential to be careful now. He couldn't see anyone. Just to be safe, Borya turned into a backstreet, then ducked into a doorway and waited. A rattle of footsteps came from behind him. He prepared himself to fight. One minute. Two minutes. No one appeared. Good.

He doubled back on himself, then turned left and then right. The streets of Kreuzberg all looked the same. Tree-lined boulevards with bulky five-story buildings on either side. You would have no idea, he thought, finally approaching the shop, the sort of stuff that went on behind these respectable looking shutters.

He looked around. The street was empty. Lunchtime was a good time to come. Berlin was at its quietest and Olezka and his men were rarely around at this time.

Even so, Borya would have to be quick.

Inside, Borya stepped over the strewn clothes which Minty used to sell for a small fortune. He knew exactly where he needed to go. The destruction continued in the back room. The carcass of Minty's sewing machine lay twisted and smashed on the floor and a filing cabinet had been emptied of its contents.

Olezka and his men had done a thorough job.

Not thorough enough, Borya hoped.

Borya pulled open the toilet door and snapped on the

light. The room was no bigger than a cupboard and contained just a toilet and sink. He stood for a few seconds and repeated Minty's instructions. The sink was on the wall to the left. It looked normal.

"Push the sink," he muttered. "Okay, push the sink."

As Borya followed Minty's instructions, he heard a click and the wall opened inwards. Borya laughed out loud as the moving wall exposed a tiny space behind it. It was used as a hiding place during the war, Minty had explained. But now it made a great place for them to put their stuff. Sure enough, hidden in the gloom, were the missing shipments.

Then Borya heard a sound that filled him with fear. The shop door jangled open.

47

Leo felt the daylight sting as he prized his eyes open. Without sitting up, he looked around. The bright walls of his hotel room were especially offensive this morning.

What time is it?

Leo rolled over and reached for his phone. *Shit.* It was just after midday. He'd been asleep the whole morning.

The previous night had been pretty intense. He'd completed the shift as the techno rumbled and the black-clad dancers stomped and swayed. Although he still had no idea what people got up to in the darkroom, his imagination now had various theories.

The investigation had progressed too. Leo knew that Minty had left the club just after the man in the green coat. Whatever the link between the two men, it built on Leo's instinct that Minty was still alive.

That was good progress for the first day. *Even Allissa couldn't have done better*, Leo thought, grinning. But all it brought so far was more questions. Most crucially: *if Minty isn't dead, then where is he, and why?*

Fifteen minutes later, his eyes just beginning to focus, Leo ordered a large flat white with a double shot from the café across the road. As he waited for the coffee to be made — steam billowed industriously from the gleaming machine on the counter — Leo checked the notes he had made from Minty's website. Minty sold clothes. Very expensive and, apparently, fashionable clothes. The unique selling point was the fabric they were made from. It was all explained on the website in flamboyant terms, but in essence, it was some kind of recycled cotton and synthetic mix that Minty had imported from South America. The website glamorously described the process and boasted that Minty was one of the only designers in Europe to use this sustainable product.

Visiting the shop was Leo's first job today. Even if it was closed — as Leo expected it to be with its proprietor missing — it may still hold the answers he needed. The shop itself, as Leo understood it, was more like a design studio. It seemed that having premises in Kreuzberg was a statement of authenticity for the fashion designers of Berlin. Hopefully, the place would help Leo better understand the man he needed to find.

On the train towards Kottbusser Tor, Leo looked around at the rooftops and brightly coloured buildings of the district. Imperial townhouses of white and red jostled for space next to 1960s concrete apartment blocks. Creepers climbed the walls and flags hung from windows and balconies. Stepping out into the afternoon sunshine, Leo had an unusual feeling — he actually quite liked Berlin. It felt quiet and calm, vibrant and fresh, almost like his familiar Brighton. Descending from the station, Leo passed a man in a grey suit talking to one in traditional Jewish robes. A young lady with tattoos and ripped jeans walked beside him. At the corner below, two women wearing gleaming, sequined headscarves gossiped. It seemed to Leo, as someone who was becoming increasingly well-travelled, that Berlin was a city of the world. With that, Leo started to understand why a young fashion designer might want to make the city the base of his operations.

Leo followed the directions on his phone to a wide and quiet street lined by white five-story townhouses. The rumble of the city had faded and, listening carefully, Leo heard birds from a nearby park. As though on cue, a pair of blackbirds perched on a windowsill a few feet above Leo. They examined Leo through small, inquisitive eyes.

Leo dug out his phone and checked the directions. He must be close now.

Yep, Minty's shop was about a hundred yards ahead on the left-hand side.

Leo squinted down the road. Most of the shops had their white shutters rolled down. Maybe early afternoon wasn't the time the fashionistas of Berlin liked to open their businesses.

Walking on, Leo counted the ascending numbers — 55, 57, 59. Minty's was 87.

One of the shops further along the road did seem to be open. Its shutter was up, and something moved behind the darkened glass. Leo quickened his pace. Maybe they would know something about Minty.

77, 79. Leo continued to count the numbers on the doors.

81, 83. *What number is Minty's again?*

Leo checked his phone. 87.

Looking a few doors up, Leo saw number 87 and stopped.

87 was the shop with the raised shutter.

87 was Minty's shop.

Leo had expected, with Minty missing, for the shop to be

shut. The place being open made no sense. Leo crossed the road. With each step, his heart beat heavily in his chest.

Leo pushed the door open and stepped inside.

The stop had been ransacked. The floor was strewed with clothes and boxes had been pushed from shelves. The sofa was flipped, and its base torn open.

Someone had clearly been here looking for something.

Leo stiffened as he heard movement from the back of the shop. What he saw next made his mouth gape in astonishment.

48

"That one looks like a castle, don't you think?" Minty says to Charles. They're lying on their backs in the garden of their family home. The smell of cut grass and wildflowers hangs in the air. It's the summer holidays — one of those heady summer holidays of childhood which seems to last forever. At least, Minty and Charles are young enough to think it will last forever. Each day is just a new adventure.

"No, it looks like a boat," Charles says, rolling over. Shoots of the freshly cut grass stick all over his clothes.

"No, it's the wrong way up to be a boat. Maybe if it was that way?"

Charles lays back and narrows his eyes. Their ears are almost touching as they lie head to head on the lawn.

"Pah, I don't know what you're on about. This one though" — Charles extends a hand to point at another of the nimbus shapes — "that's a rabbit."

"Definitely not, it's a car," Minty says, his arm following Charles' against the deep blue of the summer sky.

"It's not," Charles says, swinging his arm around to

thump Minty on the shoulder. Seeing it coming, Minty deflects it and sends another back at Charles. As the clouds — be them cars, castles, rabbits or boats — slide regally overhead, the two boys roll and whoop across the grass.

BEHIND THE WINDOW in Minty's bedroom, a cloud of an undiscernible shape floated by. Minty watched it through vacant eyes. His mind was elsewhere. The new day had done nothing to alleviate his sour mood. As the clock on the bedside table clicked into the early afternoon, Minty rolled over to face the wall. He didn't even want to see the empty room today.

His meeting with the Russian last night had been a complete waste of time.

The furrows which lined Minty's brow became deeper as he questioned why he'd gone along with the plan in the first place. Was the money really that important?

He could leave now if he accepted that he wasn't going to get money. The car was ready. It was packed with all the things they needed and parked beside the house. He could pull off the tarpaulin, start the engine, and be on his way out of the city within minutes.

The thought caused Minty to sit up. He wasn't a victim here; he was in charge of his life. He could make a choice. Fuck the money. Yes, it was a lot of money. It was enough money to set them up for the future. But was it worth the pain his family were going through?

Minty pictured his mum and dad moving morosely from room to room. They'd probably not even spoken to each other in days as they mourned their son. Then the image of his mum's grief-lined face swam into his thoughts. He could stop this all right now. He could get out of the city, forget the money, and tell his parents the truth. They deserved that. That was worth more than the money. Wasn't it?

Minty sat up straighter and looked around the room. He could put an end to this right now.

Through the window, the tree-covered slopes which led towards the abandoned listening station shimmered. *Am I just being selfish? Is the money really that important?*

He could make that much money on his own if he tried. Without all this pain. Without all this suffering.

Minty felt a surge of energy and stood up. They should go now. Forget the Russian. Forget the euros. He should get out of this city, get a safe distance away, and then call his parents.

49

Leo heard movement from the darkness at the rear of the shop. Someone was here. Beyond the fallen racks and scattered clothes, a door led into the shop's backroom. Leo squinted into the gloom but couldn't make anything out.

He heard movement again and his anxiety rose.

"Hello?" Leo said. It sounded braver than he felt.

Something scraped across the floor and a figure appeared in the doorway. Leo swallowed. He took a slow and controlled breath, hoping it would calm his welling sense of panic.

The man stepped forwards and Leo began to register his features. He was thin, slight, had close-cropped hair and wore a long green coat.

Leo recognised him. It was unmistakable, even from the grainy, late-night CCTV footage. This was the man Minty had followed from the nightclub.

"I'm... I'm... looking for Minty Rolleston," Leo said. His throat was suddenly dry. Anxiety squeezed his struggling lungs.

The man stared at Leo but didn't reply.

"Do... do you speak... speak English?" Leo managed.

"Yes." He had a Russian accent.

"I'm looking for Minty Rolleston," Leo said again, more feebly this time.

The man stepped forward. His grey-blue eyes considered Leo without blinking. "He's gone."

"Do you know where?" Leo said. "This is his shop, isn't it?"

"Listen," the Russian said, taking another step towards Leo. "I don't know who you are, and I don't want to find out."

"I... I just need to know where he's gone. That's all," Leo said, his voice shaky.

Leo saw the smaller man's knuckles ball into fists. Leo's chest tightened. He inhaled slowly.

For a fleeting moment, Leo wondered if Minty could actually be in the back room of the shop. But then, why would he be hiding out in his own shop?

"Minty's not here," the Russian said, stepping closer and looking up at Leo. Although Leo was bigger, there was something imposing about the guy. Something in the way he looked that told Leo not to mess.

"Now you go too," the man said.

Stepping backwards, Leo felt the door handle dig into his back. He tried to inhale another breath, but it wouldn't come.

Feeling the onset of panic, Leo turned, opened the door and fled back outside.

50

Despite only being inside for a couple of minutes, Leo's pulse raced. He needed to get away from this place and think about what he'd seen. Without a better plan, Leo headed back towards the metro station.

Part of him, the cowardly part, urged him to run, to get away from the balled fists and malevolent expression of the man in the green coat as quickly as possible. But he wasn't in any danger and forced himself to walk slowly. He wasn't going to overreact.

By the time he'd reached the end of the street, Leo felt calm. Then the things he knew about Minty's disappearance began to stream through his mind.

Minty had gone to a club on the night of his supposed death and left just before the man in the green coat. He'd used a clean phone to call his brother. Now the man with the green coat was in his shop.

At the corner of the street, Leo paused and looked back. Everything looked normal from this distance. But Leo knew that behind the darkened glass of number 87, something was wrong.

Leo needed to think. He needed to work out what it all meant. In the crime stories Leo had absorbed during his younger years, there was always a moment where the eccentric detective just figured something out. It just seemed to appear in a flurry of brilliance. An enlightened brainwave, and in that moment, the case that that had baffled Scotland Yard for the preceding two-hundred pages was solved. For Leo, it wasn't like that. There was no flash, no great white light, no moment of brilliance. He found that he had to drag the truth out of the mud, kicking, screaming and fighting against him all the way.

Losing focus on the street around him, Leo ran their previous cases through his mind. At this point, Leo would normally talk things through with Allissa. *Things would be better if Allissa was here,* Leo thought. Stubbornly, he fought the idea. He could do this alone. He'd found Allissa in Kathmandu; that was a lot more distant. A lot more dark and dangerous than Berlin.

Leo dug out his phone and saw that Allissa had already called. He hadn't heard it. His finger hovered over the return call button. Then he saw the man in the green coat step from Minty's shop. The man locked the door, pulled down the shutter and then started in Leo's direction. He carried a bag across one shoulder.

Leo leapt out of sight behind a wall and scurried on his hands and knees to a large tree. Leo peered out as the man approached.

Leo thought through his options. Seeing the man in the first place had been a stroke of luck. This was a link — a lead. But, as always, it just led to more unanswered questions.

As the man neared, Leo moved back around the tree to stay out of sight.

Leo had made the connection now. He could just go back to the hotel and wait for Allissa. She would be here in a few hours.

Or, he thought, his confidence growing, he could follow the man in the green coat.

As the man crossed beneath the shadow of a looming church, Leo knew he had seconds to decide. He clenched his teeth. *Follow or wait?*

Leo thought about how great it would be to find Minty before Allissa even got here. If it were the other way around, Allissa wouldn't just sit and wait for him. She'd go all in. Jump in at the deep end — one chance. Let's go. He should do the same. Definitely.

51

The departures hall buzzed with activity. Allissa had made good time on the train from London and cleared the security checkpoint quickly. Now she reclined into an uncomfortable wooden chair in one of the airport's bars and gazed at the thing she promised herself she wouldn't have — a pint of beer. She was just going to have one to take the edge off the hangover from the party last night. The hair of the dog. The cure and the cause. Just one.

But with the beer in front of her now, other worries occupied her mind. She'd tried calling Leo again, but he hadn't answered. Why hadn't she heard from him? What was happening to him over there? Was he alright?

Before now, Allissa had never been bothered if people didn't contact her. She remembered once having a conversation with a friend about the correct frequency of replying to someone's messages. Apparently, too often meant one thing, and not often enough meant something else. Allissa didn't care. If she wanted to contact someone, she did. If they didn't want to contact her back, then that was just their choice. No biggy.

So why, she thought, dropping the phone to the table beside the untouched pint, was she now so bothered Leo hadn't replied?

It's because this is a professional relationship, Allissa thought.

They were business partners. Replying to your business partner was essential in a professional relationship. You needed to keep each other in the loop, that was the deal. That was how businesses worked.

A professional relationship.

The term echoed through her mind. With it came a pang of disappointment.

Allissa looked at the empty chair across the table from her. Okay, so she missed Leo's company too. There was nothing wrong with that though, surely? Places like airports were boring on your own.

"It's a professional relationship," she muttered out loud, attracting the attention of the couple at the next table. Allissa's brow darkened further. She didn't know if she was more frustrated with Leo for not replying, or with herself for being so bothered. Reaching forward, she picked up the beer. Maybe it was just the anxiety of the hangover. She'd be fine after a few swigs of this.

52

For the first two streets, Leo kept his distance. Both streets were wide, straight and almost empty. Leo was far enough away that if the man did turn, he probably wouldn't recognise him.

After ten minutes, the man turned onto a busier road that ran straight in either direction. Four lanes of traffic rumbled past the shops and cafes which lined both sides. Picking up his pace, Leo passed dozens of bikes locked to a railing on the wide pavement. Although Leo could now get closer, activity on the busy street would also make it easier for him to lose sight of the man. He couldn't risk that happening.

Halving the distance between himself and the man, Leo stepped in time behind a pair of women walking yapping dogs. From behind their swaying figures, Leo kept his eyes on the man. He wasn't going to stop looking at him now. If the man stepped down a side street or into a building and Leo wasn't watching, he would be lost. Leo's chance would be gone.

Leo considered what he'd do when the man reached his

destination. Was it too convenient to assume he would be going directly to Minty? Probably. But wherever he was going, at least it would be another place to look; another connection in the investigation; a link that could lead to an answer.

Watching the man closely, Leo didn't notice as one of the dogs squatted beside a tree. Deep in conversation, the woman paused to let the animal have its fun. Realising just in time, Leo stepped around them.

Conscious of walking alone and unobscured, Leo quickened his pace until he caught up with a group of youngsters, probably students. They occupied the whole pavement and spoke loudly, each clutching a large-screen phone. Staying a few paces behind them, Leo fixed his gaze on the man with the green coat. He was now only thirty metres ahead.

The man paused at the roadside and looked left and right. Leo darted into a shop and watched him cross the road and disappear through a door.

After Leo was sure the man had gone inside, he ducked into a café two doors down and sat at a table in the window.

53

Minty gripped the shuddering steering wheel of the ten-year-old VW Golf and narrowed his gaze. This was it. They were going. To hell with the Russian and their plans. To hell with the money.

In one hour's time, they would be away from the city and he could make that call to his family. He would be able to put them out of their misery. Minty hoped they wouldn't hate him for it. He hoped they'd understand.

Then, after putting it all behind them, they could drive on somewhere. Maybe Spain, or Portugal. Maybe somewhere further. It didn't matter. They would just keep going until they found somewhere they liked. Or until they ran out of money. With thoughts of freedom in his mind, Minty felt his conviction dissolve. He had saved a few thousand euros in the last few months. That would be enough to get started. But what would he do when that ran out? Continue his fashion business under another name?

Thinking about the business, Minty felt a welling sadness. He had loved that business. The adventure of the creative process — not knowing what was going to come out. The thrill of someone wanting to buy it, actually wanting to part with their money for one of his designs. And the pride he felt when he saw them worn around the city. Minty remembered the first time that had happened. He was in a club, and he saw a girl wearing one of his dresses. The way she wore it took his breath away. It clung to her body in all the right places; it was effortless, stylish, perfect. She was perfect. In the rear-view mirror, he saw himself smiling.

But that was gone now. The business was gone. That wasn't to say he couldn't ever design clothes again. Of course, he could. But he'd have to start from scratch. New designs. New supplies. New distribution networks. He would have to be very careful too; any links to his old network would be dangerous.

Minty swallowed, suddenly thirsty. But that didn't matter. They'd stop in an hour.

The business was gone, and what did he have to show for it? A few thousand euros hidden beneath the carpet of a ten-year-old VW Golf. Basically, nothing. Minty exhaled. He had nothing. Sure, he could go and start again, but that was the same as wiping the last five years from the record. It would all have been for nothing.

Spotting movement further down the street, Minty slid deeper into the driver's seat. Parked on the driveway to the side of the house, and hidden behind a deciduous hedge, the car couldn't be seen easily. But Minty was cautious.

From his slumped position, he watched the people from the house next door descend their front steps and start in his direction. They were a young family; a man, a woman and two young boys. The boys must have been around three and five. The family chatted together. Minty couldn't hear

Berlin

their words but saw that whatever they were discussing had them all enthralled. They were a family. They looked happy.

Minty bit his lip. They must be doing well because the houses in this neighbourhood were expensive. He would have to sell a lot of clothes for them to live in a house like that. Or, he thought, as he felt the final bit of resolve drain from him, he would have to wait around to get his money.

54

Borya let the door bang closed behind him and looked around. He had always liked this place. Although it just looked like a run-down townhouse — the render crumbling to expose the bricks beneath and tattered posters flapping fitfully — it was one of the best secret hangouts in the city. The only thing that hinted to the constant party inside was the small window which glowed invitingly.

It reminded Borya of the Berlin he'd known many years ago. The Berlin he had moved to and never left. The city before the multiple waves of regeneration turned houses like this into swanky apartments and offices.

It felt familiar. Borya had been coming here for many years after all. Originally, the place had been a squat, occupied by people with nowhere else to go. Over the years the residents had fought off various redevelopment schemes and managed to buy the place. It was now theirs, thanks in some small part to the multiple shady deals Borya had conducted here. Now run by a small community of people, it was a nightclub, late bar and provided accommodation in the dingy rooms above for the people who worked there.

The whole place was cheap and inconspicuous, which was just what Borya needed.

Borya raised a hand at the woman behind the bar. He knew her, although her name escaped him. A pair of tourists sat at the bar, talking loudly amid a collection of glasses. The woman poured a thick orange liquid into two small glasses and pushed them towards the customers. Borya shoved through a door at the far end of the room and climbed the stairs to the first floor.

"Manuel," Borya said, stepping into the office. The man he had come to meet sat behind a paper-strewn desk.

Manuel leant back on his chair and looked up at Borya. His chubby jowls contorted into a grin.

"Ah, Borya." The man stubbed a cigarillo into an overflowing ashtray and crossed his arms. "You're a wanted man I hear. Everyone around town is looking for you."

Borya's eyes skipped left and right. The room was empty.

"Just a little trouble," Borya said, his Adam's apple bobbing. "Nothing I can't handle."

"If you're sure. You know I'll help you in any way I can. You've kept this place going for us over the years."

"Just the deal we spoke about. This will get me out of the city for a few months."

Manuel nodded. Borya liked the man. They had done many deals over the years and Borya trusted him.

"What have you got for me then?"

"Just what I promised, my friend." Borya dropped his bag to the table. "This really is the best," he said, pulling open the bag.

Manuel peered inside and then sat back. His hands knitted across his chest.

"You are making me very rich indeed," Manuel said.

Three minutes later, Borya stepped back into the bar. The deal had been quick and profitable. Borya knew he could have got more for the stuff given time. Under these circumstances, though, he didn't mind.

The two men at the bar were still slumped forward deep in conversation.

He had just one more deal to do before heading to meet Minty.

Finding himself grinning, Borya stepped out into the coming dusk.

55

Allissa walked through the sliding doors of Schönefeld Airport and out into the early evening. She still hadn't seen or heard anything from Leo. Looking at her phone, Allissa wondered whether Leo was trying to prove he could do this on his own.

What was it he'd said — *"I found you in Kathmandu, didn't I?"*

Of course, he was right. But he didn't need to search on his own anymore. They now had each other. They were in this together.

Allissa hit Leo's number and held the phone to her ear. The ringing tone sounded distant.

Allissa felt a sting of worry as, after ten rings, it cut to nothing. She hoped he wasn't in danger. She switched to the 'Find Your Phone' app she and Leo had both installed on their phones. They'd installed and tested it a few weeks ago in the flat and were impressed by its accuracy. The blue dot told Allissa that Leo was somewhere near Kreuzberg.

If he won't answer his phone, Allissa thought, *I'll just have to track him down.*

56

Leo was watching the door the man had gone through when he heard his phone vibrate on the table. He glanced at it and saw that Allissa was calling. She would have now landed in Berlin.

He picked up the phone and was just about to answer when he saw the door across the street open. The man in the green coat stepped out. Leo shot to his feet, paid for his coffee, and stuffed the phone away. He would have to talk to Allissa later.

Leo watched at the door for the man to get ahead of him and then stepped out into the falling darkness. Families now dined in brightly lit restaurants, and groups of men sat smoking outside bars. Smoke curled upwards in thick white clouds. A few of them noticed Leo as he passed. Some even followed him with their eyes, darkened to shadows by the distant streetlights.

Ahead, the man in the green coat turned right. Seeing a gap in the traffic, Leo hurried across the road and followed him. This road, like the last, was broad and busy. Lined on the right-hand side with bars and cafes, on the left, it opened onto a gloomy expanse of parkland. Music and people from one of the bars spilt onto the pavement. A peel of laughter from a group of men startled Leo as he passed.

The man in the green coat crossed the road and walked into the park. Crossing after him, Leo gazed into the gloom. The hazy sun had melted into a sky of angry red.

Another cheer from the drinkers at the bar shook Leo into action. He couldn't give up now. Clenching his fists, he took a deep breath of the cooling night air and walked into the Volkpark Hesenheide.

Despite the darkness, Berliners were still out in force. A man ran past Leo, his breath billowing in the night. Leo looked left and right for any sign of the green coat in the unquiet night. There was none. The man had melted into the gloom.

Fifty metres into the park, the city's light surrendered to the park's turbulent dusk. Leo paused and looked around. Streetlights cast the occasional island of light. Ahead, a cyclist shot through one like a moth in the night. The lawns lay in vast swathes of black. Leo squinted. Was that the sway of the green coat? He couldn't see anyone. Darkness like this could hide anything. He'd seen the man enter the park no more than two minutes ago. He must be nearby. Leo had to keep going.

Percussive heartbeats rattled between Leo's ears. He wasn't sure if it was his impending dread of the situation or some geographical peculiarity, but he now felt like he couldn't see anything at all.

Ahead of him the park's lawns sprawled through the darkness. After a few steps, Leo heard voices. Glaring into the blackness, he saw a group of ghost-like figures. They were just floating grey outlines. The orange tips of their cigarettes danced like fireflies. Leo looked for any indication the man with the green coat was there. None of them seemed the right size or shape.

Leo turned from the group and followed the path deeper into the park. Grabbing his phone, he looked at the park on the map. The park spanned numerous city blocks and included playing fields, a café, and somewhere, now buried amongst the trees, an outdoor cinema.

The night hung thick all around him. Facing back to the darkness again, Leo heard something move. It was close, but he couldn't see it. He resisted the urge to use the light from his phone.

It moved again. Then slowly, insidiously, a person came into view, a tall, thin man whose eyes glimmered from some distant light. It wasn't the man Leo had followed. This man was too tall.

Leo's anxiety rose. His muscles stiffened, and tightness consumed his chest.

"Möchtest du etwas?" the man said.

Somewhere behind the man, Leo sensed more movement. They weren't alone.

"I'm... I'm..." Leo stuttered, his voice weak. He breathed deeply. He tried to control the panic which burned his chest and stung his vision. Each muscle attempted to fight against the temptation to run.

"You want something?" The man spoke again, switching to English.

Breathe in and out. Focus. Calm.

"You want hashish? Charlie?"

"No, I..." Leo's thick tongue stumbled over the words.

Then Leo spotted something through the darkness. A

figure moved, swaying towards them through the trees. It was just a dark shape in the gloom, but the height and build were right.

"I need to see Minty Rolleston," Leo said, loud enough for the figure in the darkness to hear.

"You want Charlie?" the man repeated. In the gloom behind the man, Leo saw the figure had stopped moving.

"I'm looking for a man called Minty Rolleston," Leo said again. "His parents sent me to find him."

As Leo spoke a light appeared. It was nothing more than a small torch, but it stung Leo's eyes as it shone towards him. A voice followed in a thick Russian accent.

"How do you know Minty Rolleston?"

Around Leo, shapes melted and formed from the darkness. The first man disappeared, and a smaller shadow surfaced from the gloom. Leo squinted against the light. Leo fought to keep his breathing under control.

"His parents have sent me to look for him," Leo said.

From somewhere nearby, an animal called out, though the sound was quickly lost beneath the bullying growl of the city.

"His family sent you?" The Russian's inflexion didn't make it clear whether it was a question or a statement. Leo nodded, still dazed by the bright beam of the torch.

"You come from Brighton?" the speaker asked. Closer now.

Again, Leo nodded.

A bike clattered past them. Although its rider was an invisible force in the darkness, the light attached to its handlebars illuminated the man for a moment. Leo got a flash of the green coat, the thin pale face, the closely cropped hair.

"Yes, I come from Brighton," Leo said.

"Minty's parents sent you?" the man asked again. Leo found his use of Minty's first name reassuring. The muttered words that followed reassured him further. "He said they would be worried about him. I can see why..." the man trailed off.

Leo focused on the man. Did this mean he had spoken to Minty?

"Well?" the man said, snapping his focus back onto Leo and shaking the torch. "Minty's parents send you, yes?"

"Yes," Leo said quickly.

"What's the name of his brother?"

"Charles Rolleston," Leo said. "He came to see me a few days ago. He said that the family was suspicious about his death and wanted me to find out what had happened."

"I don't believe you." The beam of light held steady. "I think you are working with them. Is a very clever plan. Get an Englishman to pretend. Very clever. But not clever enough."

"Wait," Leo said. "Listen to this." Leo scrolled through his phone and selected the recording he'd made from Charles' answerphone. "This is the message Minty left on Charles' answerphone on the night he was supposed to have died."

Leo pressed play. Minty's voice strained from the phone's small speaker. The beam of light held steady.

"I'm just here to see what happened to him," Leo said after Minty's voice on the recording had trailed off into the noise of the rumbling train. "His family are very concerned."

"You are alone?"

"Yes," Leo said.

Leo felt the man grab his bicep. The Russian said nothing as he began to pull Leo through the darkness.

"What? Wait, where are we going?" Leo yelled.

The Russian stopped and pulled a phone from the folds of his coat. He barked a few words into it and then turned to Leo.

"We are going to see Minty Rolleston, of course."

57

Anafisa sat behind the wheel of her Maserati Levante and looked at her phone. She'd just received the call she was waiting for. The call to go and pick up Borya. She tapped the steering wheel with her thumb. Was she really going to do this?

She liked Borya. Their time together had been good.

She also liked her fingers still attached to her hands, though. And she liked money.

She was in Olezka's debt, and this would set the record straight. And it would give her a nice little pay packet too. Anafisa looked at herself in the rear-view mirror. Beneath the makeup, she was tired. That money could make her life a whole lot easier, that was for sure.

Anafisa thumbed the screen of the phone and held it to her ear.

"Borya has just called," Anafisa said. "I'm collecting him now and taking him to Teufelsberg. He's meeting Minty Rolleston there."

Anafisa heard Olezka mutter.

"I can see your man behind me already." Anafisa

glanced across the street. The black Jeep was still there. "He can follow me if he wants, but do you really want Borya getting any more suspicious?"

"Okay, okay," Olezka grumbled. He spoke to someone in the background.

"Olezka, after this I owe you nothing more. My debt is paid."

Anafisa ended the call and started the Maserati.

58

The man let go of Leo's arm when they got back to the road. Leo thought about running. He could disappear back into the park or out into the city in seconds. But then he wouldn't find out where Minty was.

The noise of the city was louder here. Music thudded from the bar across the road and traffic growled around them. Leo watched the man pull the phone out again and give some instructions. He spoke in Russian. The phone he used was a simple, low-tech handset. A "burner." There was only one reason someone would use a phone like that. The man in the green coat didn't want to be traced.

A large, red car emerged from the stream of traffic and mounted the kerb ahead. Leo recognised the trident of the Maserati logo.

"Come now," the Russian said, walking toward the car.

Leo glanced at the man.

"Get in."

Leo took a deep breath and opened the door. This man knew where Minty was. Leo didn't have a choice.

The car smelled of tobacco smoke and sweet air freshener. With the doors closed, the sounds of the city sank to a whisper.

The driver was a woman with long dark hair. She examined Leo in the mirror, then pulled out into the traffic. A bus behind them was forced to brake and protested with horns and lights.

"What's... where are we going?" Leo asked.

Without replying to Leo, the Russian spoke to the driver, who passed back a white pipe.

"We're going to see Minty," the Russian said. "He's in a safe place."

The man packed the pipe with tobacco, then lit it.

"They used to say," — the Russian looked out at the passing city — "that the night was darker in the East. I'm not sure anymore." He took a drag on the pipe and exhaled through the window. "I have lived in this city almost my whole life... I have lived here and worked here. I feel like I have fought my own battles for this city."

The Maserati made quick progress through the quiet streets.

"But it's time for a change around here," the Russian said, exhaling again. "I'm sorry, how rude of me. I have not even introduced myself. I am Borya."

Leo took the hand and introduced himself. Borya's grip was firm and dry.

"Now, we're friends," Borya said. "It's okay. You're here to help Minty. You're a friend of ours. You have nothing to worry about."

Leo didn't feel so sure.

Borya said something to the driver and they both laughed.

"Where are we going?" Leo asked again. The darkened buildings of the city had thinned out into suburban sprawl.

Borya rubbed his hands together. The pipe remained clenched between his teeth. "Minty is in a place no one will ever find him. They wouldn't even think to look."

"Why does he want people to think he's dead?"

"You will see my friend, you will see. All will be explained. You have nothing to worry about," Borya repeated.

Borya pulled a bag from between his legs and put it on the seat between them. Then the driver passed another bag from the passenger seat. Borya opened the first bag and started removing bundles of money. Leo watched him. He could only imagine why a man would be carrying that much money around.

When Borya had divided the money, he passed one of the bags back to the driver, who stuffed it beneath the passenger seat. Borya kept the other on the seat beside him.

The silence was suddenly broken when the driver shouted and pointed her finger at the rear-view mirror. Borya exploded with energy. His jaw tensed, and his previous grey pallor became an angry red.

"We are being followed," he snarled. "I knew they were suspicious. But to follow me? We must try to lose them," Borya shouted at the driver. "Lose them now!"

59

Allissa noticed the sign for the U-Bahn at Kottbusser Tor. That's where it happened. That's where Minty was supposed to have fallen, jumped, or been pushed in front of a train. She still hadn't heard from Leo. This was not the way Allissa liked to do things. If a case came up like this again, they would go together or not at all.

Zipping up her coat against the coming chill of the evening, Allissa walked from the station's raised iron structure. Behind her somewhere, another train shuddered to a shop, and a roar of footsteps headed her way.

The early evening was busy. People walked home from work or headed out for the evening. Laughter erupted from a group sat outside a café.

Allissa flicked to the 'Find Your Phone' app and sighed. The blue dot was now on the other side of the city. If Leo wanted to do this all on his own, then he should have just said that. She didn't need to be following him around Europe for no reason.

She headed to a nearby line of taxis and got in the first one. Maybe he was doing so well he didn't need her at all. Maybe she should just leave him to it. She could go and see the girls in Kathmandu, or perhaps go somewhere completely new.

60

The next moment, two things happened at once. First, Borya fired a string of serrated words, and the driver accelerated hard. The Maserati, which had been purring softly so far, sprung forwards. Leo tried turning to see the vehicle behind them but was pinned deep into the seat. From the lights which strobed through the rear window, it looked as though it was very close.

Beside Leo, Borya shouted and gesticulated wildly with his pipe. Tobacco scattered on the seats around him.

"We must lose them," Borya shouted. "They cannot follow us."

Leo looked from Borya to the driver. The Maserati filled with the xenon of their pursuer's headlights. Leo felt his pulse jolt.

He knew he shouldn't have trusted the Russian. Now he was involved in some kind of gang war car chase.

Leo felt the pit of his stomach drop as the car squealed around a corner. His muscles tightened further. He fought for breath.

The driver increased her speed on a straight stretch of road. Ahead, an intersection lay empty. A green traffic light hung above the carriageway.

The driver buried the pedal and the Maserati shot forwards. Borya tensed.

The traffic light flicked from green to orange. The outline of a smirk played across Borya's thin lips.

Leo snatched a breath. Each one became more futile and pathetic.

Then, in slow motion, the traffic light wavered from orange to red. An angry, violent red. A warning. The tarmac, the waiting cars and the pale face of the Russian glowed in the ferocious hue.

Borya shouted and pointed with his free hand.

The car behind continued to bare down on them. Headlights cut through the rear window.

Leo felt a change in speed.

Were they slowing? Was it over?

A moment of relief.

Then, Leo was pushed into the seat as they accelerated for the changing lights.

Fifty metres away.

The driver accelerated for the intersection.

Forty metres.

Borya screamed.

Thirty metres away.

Traffic from the left started creeping into the intersection. The first car, accelerating quickly on the empty road, sped from right to left. Then the snout of a truck began creeping forward. Its engine strained to move the heavy load. Large tyres rolled.

Twenty metres.

The Maserati swerved.
The lights behind them dimmed.
Leo stopped breathing.
A flash of light. Horns. Tyres on tarmac. The hard thump of Leo's pulse in his ears. Then, nothing.

61

Minty's family had always been important to him. Although they didn't see each other that often, with him living in Berlin and them near Brighton, they talked frequently. The four of them — his mum, dad and brother — had wicked senses of humour and often shared jokes or funny pictures. Minty missed them desperately.

He pulled open the back door and looked out into the night. From the back garden, he could make his way straight into the woods. If anyone happened to be watching the front — which was unlikely but possible — they wouldn't see anything.

Minty looked back into the house. It was the sort of place he had once dreamed about living in. But, in the last few days, it had brought him no happiness. Pacing the marble-tiled hallways, sinking into the large sumptuous chairs, or even lounging in the bath — which at the press of a button produced bubbles — had not touched the thick fog of worry that hung around him. And all the time the question was not far away: what had he done? What pain was he causing his family?

Stepping out into the darkness, Minty shivered again. Tonight, he was going to put it right. Tonight, whatever happened, he would leave Berlin, and by the time the sun came up tomorrow, he would have spoken to his family.

Pulling the black hat down over his ears, Minty turned deeper into the woodland. He had been so close to going earlier. So close to leaving and forgetting all about the money. But he had come this far, and he couldn't do it.

He had caused so much pain and suffering already, that to leave now without the money would mean it was all in vain.

The finger of light from his torch swept through the trees.

It wasn't just the money, though. It was security. Security that was quickly becoming important to him. The problem was, Minty had no control over the situation. He was totally in Borya's grip.

Minty tried to think of how he had given up so much of his freedom. He'd got greedy; that was the problem. In the early days, the sizeable cash payments had been a bonus. They'd helped him keep the business afloat and support the lifestyle he'd wanted. But then he'd got used to them, so when they were doubled, he accepted the extra money gladly. Before long, most of his income came in the shady packages left in the backroom of his shop. At that point, there was nothing he could do. He was reliant. He was addicted.

Minty inhaled the cold night air. It was that greed that had got him here. Greed that had trapped him in a cycle of dangerous money and unnecessary spending. Greed that was now causing unimaginable pain to his friends and family back at home.

Minty would put it right... if it wasn't too late.

The moment they were safe, he'd make that call. But until then, what could he do?

As the incline began to steepen, Minty visualised the coming hours. It was all going to end tonight. Borya would arrive with the money. Minty would climb back down the hill, get in the car, start the engine, and pull out of the drive. He would never come back.

62

"Ha! That will show you!" Borya shouted at the rear window as the Maserati continued barreling down the road.

Leo opened his eyes slowly. Had they made it?

The last thing he remembered was the flash of the truck's lights. Its impenetrable silver grill, and then... Then they were through.

"Messing with us! Ha! Fuckers!" Borya shouted again.

Leo unfurled himself on the seat. His back and shoulders ached from the tension. "Who was that? What did they want?" he asked, his voice shaking.

"Don't you worry about that." Borya began to restock his pipe. "It's okay. It's almost sorted."

Borya lit the pipe again.

Leo glanced at his phone. There was a message from Allissa. Stealing a glance at Borya, Leo decided he shouldn't read it now. He couldn't risk the Russian thinking he was passing on their location or something. Anyone who used a burner phone and was driven around in a Maserati must be up to something dodgy.

The Maserati slowed to a purr and turned off the main road.

"That was some excellent driving, wasn't it?" Borya said.

Leo nodded and attempted a smile.

"Seven-litre engine in this beast," Borya said as he tapped the door. "You'd have to be quick to keep up with us."

They were now passing through an area of large, detached houses. Leo glanced at one; the enormous windows hinted at opulence within. No one would notice a Maserati snaking through this neighbourhood.

"They've got nothing on us," Borya said. He exhaled smoke through the window. "We'll be done before they've worked out where we're going. That's what it takes to succeed. You've got to do what other people won't. To risk what they can't. Go places they wouldn't expect."

The car slowed for a tight corner and began to climb. The houses had now disappeared, and trees surrounded the road. Absolute darkness hung beyond the beam of the Maserati's headlights.

"Where are we?" Leo asked. The driver shifted gears to take another sharp bend.

"We use this place for our meetings," Borya said. "It's not far."

Leo stared into the woodland as they continued to climb. He searched for a glimmer of light or some other indication of where they were. He couldn't see anything.

The Maserati slowed as they approached an iron gate blocking the road. Borya exchanged some Russian words with the driver and opened the door.

"We're here," Borya said, stepping out from the car.

63

Allissa watched the buildings of Berlin became more and more sparse as the taxi headed out of the city. Using mime and the driver's basic English, she had been able to explain she needed to follow the blue dot on the screen of the phone. The driver's face had twisted into a conspiratorial smirk at the unusual request. Allissa didn't know if it was genuine excitement for this sort of job or the prospect of a wild goose chase for which she would be paying. The journey had already taken them twenty minutes. Allissa tried not to watch the metre as it ticked beyond the thirty-euro mark.

Focusing on her phone, Allissa noticed the blue dot had stopped. She pointed at it, and the driver nodded. It was in an area of woodland on the outskirts of the city. What business did these people have taking Leo out there?

Numerous ideas pounded through Allissa's mind. None of them were good.

It was unusual for Allissa to feel the grind of worry. She hadn't experienced it in a long time. Of course, she'd cared about the women she'd helped in Kathmandu. She'd cared about Isobel and Mrs Yee in Hong Kong, both of whom now had better lives because of what Allissa had done. But this was different. Allissa had wanted to help those people because she knew it was the right thing to do. But Leo was different. Not knowing whether Leo was safe or not caused a lump to form in her chest.

"How long?" she growled at the driver.

"Zehn, urrr, ten," he replied.

64

The driver slid down the window and handed Borya a torch. Borya snapped it on.

"Leave your phone with Anafisa," Borya said, turning to Leo. "We can't risk anything here."

Leo was about to argue, but something in Borya's stare told him not to. He took out his phone and passed it through the window to Anafisa.

"I'll look after it for you," she said, adding a wink.

Borya turned and walked towards the gate.

Leo followed the billowing green coat. Borya pulled open the gate and stepped through.

"It's all about going to places that others wouldn't think of," Borya said, walking up a concrete road which opened into a larger space as the incline flattened. In the sweeping torchlight, Leo saw darkened concrete structures standing all around them. "They'd just never think to look here," Borya said. He focused the beam on the concrete tower before them.

"Where are we?" Leo asked

"Teufelsberg," Borya replied. "It means Devil's Mountain. It's made from the rubble of buildings destroyed in the war. Because West Berlin was an island, they couldn't take it very far, so it was brought here. Millions of tonnes, just piled up then covered with earth and trees."

Borya walked around a dilapidated digger covered in brightly coloured paint.

"But that's not the interesting part," Borya said. "When the Americans were looking for somewhere to listen to Russian communications, they chose here. No one trusted anyone in those days, all that spying. You see this..." Borya angled the powerful torch upwards. In the milky darkness, Leo saw two white domes high on top of concrete towers. "This is what they used to listen. To pick up radio signals, that sort of thing. No one knew what they were doing up here. Now it makes the perfect place for us too, know what I mean?" Borya turned and shot Leo a look with those cold, blue-grey eyes. "We can do what we like on the hill of the devil."

Borya opened a large metal door. It creaked on ancient hinges. "This way," he said, his voice echoing from the bare concrete walls.

Leo followed. Around them, like much of Berlin, the walls were covered with graffiti. To the right, someone's initials appeared beneath a phrase in a language Leo couldn't read.

Water dripped somewhere.

Borya led them up a staircase in the centre of the building. The resonant echo of their footsteps pounded like rain as they climbed. Leo tried to estimate how far they'd climbed. Two or three storeys perhaps.

Ahead, the stairwell opened out. Leo felt the night-time air against his face again. Reaching the top, Borya stepped forward into the space. He shone his torch left and right. It took Leo a few moments to notice the view. They looked out above the canopy of trees. Down the hillside, treetops glimmered beneath the pale moonlight, and beyond, the city gleamed like a restless ocean. Leo recognised the red and white needle of the Television Tower at Alexanderplatz flickering into the sky.

"Good view, yeah," Borya said as Leo took a tentative step forward. He wasn't going to get too close to the edge. The railing looked flimsy, and he knew they were high above the ground. High enough not to go too close.

Then, from behind them, Leo heard a voice. It was a voice he recognised.

65

"Who's this?" came the voice from behind them. It was a voice Leo had listened to hundreds of times. Even before turning, he knew who it was. He had found Minty Rolleston.

"What sort of a greeting is that?" Borya said, spinning his torch towards the voice. "I bring you something, and that's how you greet me. That's the problem with helping people, Leo, they never really appreciate it."

Minty bristled at the words. It didn't look as though the two were friends.

"Who is this?" Minty repeated, sounding out each word individually.

"This" — Borya replied, mimicking Minty's accent — "is Leo. Leo has been sent here to look for you by your parents. He was snooping around today. So I figured, as you're so worried about your family, I'd show him you're okay, and then he can tell them the truth. Then you can stop being" — Borya's voice became deep and angry — "such an ungrateful *ublyudok.*"

"Get that light out my eyes," Minty said, shading his face

with a hand.

Borya dipped the light and Leo looked Minty up and down. Although dressed in dark, nondescript clothes with a hood pulled up, he was clearly Minty Rolleston. Alive and well. Living and breathing. Beneath the hood, Minty's beard was unkempt and his brow furrowed in concern.

"How do you know he's not one of them?" Minty said finally, with less conviction than before.

"Pahahha!" Borya laughed upwards, opening his throat to the sky.

Leo looked at Minty. The designer shifted his weight from one foot to the other.

Borya leaned forward, his hands on his knees, continuing to laugh.

"Well?" Minty said, frustration growing. "How do you know he's not working with them?"

"How do I know?" Borya split into laughter again. "How do I know he's not working with a Russian gang?"

"Yes?"

"Four reasons," Borya said, immediately serious. "Number one, look at him. No Russian gangster would dress like that. Look at that hair. So untidy. It just wouldn't happen."

Leo felt Minty's eyes sweep across his body. Whether he agreed or not, the fashionista didn't argue.

"Second, on ne govorit po russki."

Leo and Minty looked blankly at each other.

"He doesn't speak Russian," Borya said.

"How do you know? He could be pretending."

"You should have heard some of the things we were saying about him in the car on the way here. No Russian would be able to — we were only joking though."

"Number three" — Borya held up three fingers — "he

has a recording of your answerphone message to your brother." Borya mimicked the designer again. "Don't lose faith, rah rah rah."

"And fourth?" Minty grumbled.

"Fourth, Olezka's men tried to follow us here —"

"They what!"

"Relax! We lost them for dust. They have no idea where we are."

"But that means they're on to us?"

"Yes, but that's okay, it's no problem. Borya has it all sorted."

Minty frowned.

"Listen, you said yesterday that you wanted your family to know. You said you were worried about them. This is your opportunity to tell them."

"You're from Brighton?" Minty said. It wasn't a question.

Leo nodded.

"What part?"

Leo thought it was an unusual time to start talking about the city.

"What part of Brighton do you live in?"

"In Hove, two streets back from Brunswick Square."

Minty nodded. "And my parents have sent you? I thought they might send someone. This was the reason I didn't want to do this." He turned on Borya. "But you said this would take just one day. I should have been out of here by now. But I'm waiting for you, holed up with nothing to do, my family worrying about me."

"Well, now your family will know you're alright. And you'll have all this money to enjoy." Borya held up the bag.

Minty reached for it.

"No no, don't snatch," Borya said, pulling the bag away.

"Just show me," Minty said.

"You guys just have no, how you say... decorum." Borya dropped the bag, squatted down and pulled open the zip. Then he pushed it across the floor towards Minty. "There you go. All yours, my friend."

Minty knelt, pulled a torch from his pocket and snapped it on. The beam felt blinding in the dark building. Borya turned to face the smouldering outline of Berlin on the horizon.

"It's a shame," Borya said. "We could have cleaned up here. This could have just been the start. This money could have been the first of many."

Minty pulled a wad of notes from the bag. They glimmered as he spun them in the light. "I assume it's all here?"

"What do you take me for?" Borya spun to face Minty. "Of course it is."

"Well, that's it then." Minty dropped the notes and zipped up the bag. Slinging it across his shoulder, he lifted it from the floor. Leo watched as the bag's fabric bulged.

"Are you sure you don't want to be a part of this business?" Borya turned to face the city again. "It's been good to work with you. Do you want to reconsider? I could make you a very wealthy man."

"No. I never wanted to be part of it in the first place. Now I'm getting out." Minty turned. "Remember the deal? Whatever you do now, my name stays out of it."

"Yes yes, but why the rush all the time? Business is as much about the people as it is the money. Don't people realise that anymore —"

"This is not business."

"Oh, it is," Borya said, pointing a finger at Minty. "This has always been business. Business is business. Whether it's fashion or drugs." He rested the finger on Minty's chest. "Or even murder."

66

Anafisa turned the Maserati around and killed the engine. For now, Borya needed to think things were going his way. If he saw the car's tail lights fading into the woodland, then he'd know something was off. Anafisa drummed her fingers on the steering wheel. This whole thing was making her nervous.

She looked at herself in the rear-view mirror. Was it possible that she was even more nervous than the night before her husband had died? There had been no reason for her to be nervous that night though. The plan was flawless. He would always go skiing before breakfast when they were staying in the Alps. And the boring bastard took the same route every day.

The simplicity of Anafisa's plan was genius. She strung a cord between two trees on her husband's route. When he didn't return, she went looking for him — like any good wife would.

She removed the cord and then raised the alarm about his crumpled body.

Obviously, his family had suspected her, but nothing

could be done. The will was signed, and skiing was known to be dangerous.

"Stupid man, had it coming to him," Anafisa said to herself in the silent car.

Then she'd moved to Berlin and her life had changed forever. Looking at the bag on the passenger seat, Anafisa wondered whether she should just take the money now and run. She could drive straight out of the city, right now. But did she really want to spend the next few years looking over her shoulder? No, that wasn't worth it. She would take her share and Olezka could have his. It was worth keeping these people on side.

She glanced at the clock on the dash. Borya had only been gone two minutes. How this was going to play out, Anafisa had no idea, but she was going to wait and see.

Anafisa opened the bag and looked at the money. Great dirty piles stacked together with elastic bands. She did some quick calculations and stashed what she assumed was a hundred thousand beneath the seat.

She drummed her fingers on the steering wheel and looked at the clock again. Borya would still be a while yet. Anafisa remembered the coke she'd found in Keal's room yesterday. She rummaged through her handbag and held it up to the light. The powder glistened.

She was impressed. She'd had it overnight and still had loads left. Maybe she didn't have such a problem with it after all. Maybe she could be trusted just to have a bit now and again.

The beasts of her addiction began to rage with the thought.

She could have a little bit now. Nothing was going to happen for the next few minutes at least.

Anafisa rolled a cigarette and sprinkled it with a greedy dose of cocaine.

A few months ago, someone had asked Anafisa why she took so many drugs. It seemed like a silly question at the time. She remembered actually laughing when they asked. That was like asking why a fish swam. It was what she was born to do.

The question had made Anafisa think, though. What was it she liked about the drugs?

It took her a while to figure it out. But when she did it just seemed obvious.

Nothing.

That's right. Nothing.

She liked the drugs because for once, she was able to think about nothing. Anafisa felt that she had always been on the go. She was always racing from one place to the next. Always trying to do something or be somewhere or escape from something. Whether it was an overbearing husband or her debt to Olezka, there was always something...

The drugs stopped that. They were a release. The ultimate release.

Anafisa put the cigarette between her lips, grabbed the lighter from the passenger seat, lit up and inhaled. Anafisa inhaled so hard her cheeks drew inwards. It looked as though she was trying to pull not just the smoke, but the whole contents of the cigarette into her lungs. That was probably true. She looked down at the cigarette's flaming end in her right hand. She just needed to get this into her body as quickly as possible.

Anafisa held the smoke for a few seconds. It felt as though it were seeping into every sinew and synapse. Then, she exhaled. A delicious, luxurious cloud of smoke poured from her nose and mouth.

Anafisa closed her eyes and enjoyed the tingle of warmth. This was it. This was why she'd let herself get close to Borya and Keal, and why she'd built up such a big debt to Olezka. This was the stuff. This was what Anafisa needed.

Running her hand across the car door, Anafisa found the button and slid the windows down. The cool night air tumbled in and cleared the smoke. This was it. This was the best.

At first, like everyone, Anafisa had snorted it. Lined it up on glass or mirrors and snorted through notes or straws. Dug it out of a dirty packet with keys or cards. Filthy. Disgusting. Inefficient.

Borya had been the one to show her that smoking it was the way. No mess. No Fuss. And smoking took the hit straight to the brain. Within seconds you were dancing with it. Borya knew the way.

As the tingle subsided and the colours drained from her vision, Anafisa put the cigarette to her lips again. She drew a deep breath, expecting to feel the warm, thick smoke fill her lungs once more. Nothing.

She tried again. Still nothing.

Anafisa opened her eyes and looked at the cigarette. It had gone out.

Mudak! Where was that lighter?

Anafisa blinked in an attempt to focus, and looked around. She ran her hand across the leather upholstery of the passenger seat — nothing. Checked her lap — nope. Ran her fingers across the car's central console — not there. She glanced down and saw it on the floor between her feet. Anafisa grabbed it, flipped open the lid and re-lit the cigarette. Then, with a smile, she placed it back between her lips.

Ahhhhh!

Colours bubbled across her mind. A tingle flew across her skin. This was it — the calm, beautiful nothingness of a drug-induced haze.

Outside the car, everything was reduced to zero. The dark woodland — she didn't notice that. The mumbling city — that was none of her concern. Whatever happened between Borya and Olezka up here on this bleak evening — Anafisa didn't care about that.

She didn't even notice the dark figure standing fifty metres from the car. She didn't notice the figure draw a pistol and screw a silencer into place. Anafisa paid no attention.

As the figure crossed towards the Maserati, Anafisa was clinging to the last tingles of the high. And as the figure raised the gun in one gloved hand and cradled it with the other, Anafisa was swimming in the nothingness of addiction. As the silencer made a whisper of the gunshot, Anafisa, in a way, got what she always wanted.

Anafisa got to think of nothing. Forever.

"Trying to fuck with me," Olezka said, sliding the gun back beneath his jacket. "That will teach the bitch."

67

Minty exhaled as his hand closed around the strap of the bag. He had the money. He pictured himself, just a few minutes from now, getting back to the house — no concern about being followed this time as they wouldn't be staying long — getting into the car and driving out of the city.

He'd done it. He was set for life.

Borya was still talking beside him, although Minty didn't hear. He was already enjoying the spoils of the bag's contents.

Then, everything changed.

From the dark stairwell came a voice which made the blood in Minty's veins run cold.

"You thought you could just fuck us over, did you?"

Something thumped deep inside Minty's skull. The ground felt as though it was moving. Through blurred vision, he tried to peer into the darkness. Dark shapes moved somewhere beyond the light.

Although he couldn't yet see the voice's owner, he knew who it was.

"Now you've made me come all this way just to get what's mine."

A shadow stepped from the gloom.

Minty's head pounded. His stomach bubbled. His legs begged to run. With blanching knuckles, he clutched the bag's handle.

There was nowhere to go. The voice was coming from the building's only stairwell.

Borya's expression melted from shock to fear.

"Stop now and drop that."

Borya's hand, which had been creeping inside the green coat, froze.

The light of a powerful torch snapped on.

"Take the gun out and drop it," the intruder said, stepping further forward. Borya stood rigid. Minty watched a flicker of a dilemma on Borya's pale complexion. Fight or flight?

Minty tried to look at the intruder but was dazzled by the bright torchlight. He could just make out the man's wide silhouette. The shape filled him with fear. One man at the back held the light while the other advanced further forwards.

Minty's eyes narrowed at the approaching figure. He looked for anything to reassure him it wasn't the man he feared.

The man stepped closer again. He had some kind of night vision device strapped across his eyes. He pushed the goggles up with a gloved hand.

Minty's stomach lurched as he recognised the man.

Olezka. He was the man in charge. He was the man who had first approached Minty and offered him more money — more than he had ever imagined — just to accept a few parcels. And the man who, when Minty planned to leave, told him what would happen if he did.

Minty tried to swallow. His tongue lay thick in his mouth.

Olezka lowered the gun and squeezed the trigger. The silencer muted the gunshot to a rumour of conflict elsewhere. Olezka's strong arm handled the recoil in practised efficiency. The next thing Minty heard was a cry from Borya. The noise echoed fitfully around the concrete and out into the night.

The hissing bullet had grazed the outside of Borya's left thigh. Borya dropped to his knees, clutching the wound with his left hand.

"Push your gun across the floor now," Olezka said, his voice little more than a whisper. The gun was now levelled at Borya's head. "The next shot will not be so kind."

Minty stared at the man. This was not supposed to be happening.

Borya swore and fished his gun from beneath the coat. Holding it by the muzzle, he placed it down on the concrete. He took deep, ragged breaths. He breathed through the pain.

"This way." Olezka indicated with his free hand.

Borya shoved the gun across the concrete as directed. Minty glanced down at it. It wasn't far away but would be useless without a steady and experienced hand to fire it.

Across Olezka's thick lips, he saw the beginnings of a smile.

68

Allissa looked down at her phone as the taxi pulled up a dark, tree-lined road. The blue dot was now just a few hundred metres away. The taxi turned a corner and slowed. Its sharp headlights scanned the woodland on either side of the road.

Allissa looked out into the darkness and wished she'd brought a torch. The light from her phone would be no match for the uninterrupted darkness here. Two cars parked on the road ahead came into view. Both were dark and appeared empty. One was a black Rolls Royce and the other was something red and sporty.

According to the blue dot on Allissa's phone, Leo was in one of those cars.

Allissa pulled some notes from her bag and counted them out for the driver. She barely registered how much the journey cost.

Allissa got out, the taxi spun on the narrow road and began to descend. She suddenly felt very alone in the soundless woodland as the brake lights disappeared.

Over the last few months, Leo and Allissa had been in

many challenging and terrifying situations. At the time Allissa had done what she needed to get them out safely. She felt that, around Leo, she had become a braver version of herself. It was as though he inspired her to be courageous. He gave her a reason to be bold.

Switching on her phone's light, Allissa began climbing towards the cars. The silver trim of the Rolls Royce sparkled. Standing a few feet away, Allissa looked again at the map. Using two fingers, she zoomed in. According to the app, Leo was inside the red car. At least his phone was.

Allissa walked around the car. The small light from her phone washed the interior in a ghostly glow. It looked empty.

"Leo, you in here?" Allissa whispered. No reply — *of course there was no reply.*

Allissa peered through the back passenger door. The car looked empty from here.

Allissa tried the door. It was locked.

Moving back to the front passenger door, Allissa tried that too. Locked as well.

Allissa bent and peered in through the passenger window. The glass was covered with something. Allissa couldn't work out what it was in the weak light from her phone.

She moved to the front and looked through the windscreen.

It took a few moments for Allissa to realise what she was looking at.

Bile bubbled in her stomach, making her retch. Allissa stepped away from the car, her hands covering her face.

There was a dead body in the driver's seat.

69

Allissa ignored bubbling nausea and rushed around to the driver's door. Panicked thoughts of Leo raged through her mind. It couldn't be him. It just couldn't be.

Reaching the driver's window, Allissa peered inside. The glass was down. The front of the car was a mess.

It was a woman. Her dark hair was matted with blood and her chin sank towards her chest. It wasn't Leo.

Allissa stepped back and took a deep breath of the cool woodland air.

It wasn't Leo. She didn't know who it was, but it wasn't Leo.

Allissa felt another wave of sickness and turned away from the gruesome scene.

What was Minty involved in?

A dead body in a car in this remote woodland.

Allissa looked back at the car. The body seemed obvious now she knew it was there. The windows and upholstery were spattered with blood. Allissa was no expert, but it can't have happened long ago. The blood on the glass still looked fresh.

But Leo's phone was in this car too. At least that's what the location app told her.

Maybe he was in the...

Allissa spat the acidic taste from her mouth and walked to the back of the car. There was only one more place he could be. The boot. She needed to check the boot.

Allissa found the handle, but it wouldn't budge. Locked. She banged on the top and listened. If someone was inside, maybe they'd try to bang back.

Allissa's sense of dread grew further. She needed to look inside.

Allissa went back to the driver's door and looked inside for the keys or the boot release switch. She tried to ignore the body.

Blood pooled into the leather and dripped onto the floor.

The car keys hung from the ignition.

Allissa forced herself not to look at the body as she reached in and slid out the keys.

The dead woman's keys felt cold.

Allissa straightened up and walked to the back of the car. She pressed a button on the key and the boot's lock disengaged. Allissa drew a deep breath and lifted the lid.

A small light blinked on.

There was a toolbox, a can of oil and some de-icer. But no body. No Leo.

Allissa felt a wave of relief.

Then she heard a cry. A loud, shrill, muscle-tensing scream of pain. It came from somewhere behind her.

Allissa spun around and looked up at the buildings beyond the gate.

They were obviously not as empty as they looked. Someone must be in there.

Allissa took a step towards the gate and then paused. She would need a weapon too. Something. Anything was better than bare hands against an armed killer.

Grabbing the toolbox, Allissa pulled open the lid and rummaged through. She removed a tyre iron — a foot-long rod of hard, solid metal — and thumped it with one hand into the palm of the other. That would do.

70

"How did you think you would get away with stealing from me?" Olezka continued. He was speaking in English. No doubt so Leo and Minty could understand.

"And now you've got these two involved," he continued. "Whatever happens to them will be on your dirty hands." Olezka waved the gun to indicate Leo and Minty, then turned to face Minty. "That whole jumping under the train thing. That was pretty good. Clever. But we know people too." Olezka was acting as though he had already won. He appeared to be enjoying himself. "If you had really died, we'd have known about it."

Borya didn't reply. Blood seeped through his fingers.

"Ambition, that's your problem," Olezka said, facing Borya. "I give you everything. A great life. More money than you could ever want. The girls. The drugs. You have it all. But that's not good enough. You want to do it your own way. You think if you stop my supply and give yourself a good payday in the process, you can get rid of me. Cut the head from the snake, so they say. I might be old, but I'm no fool."

Borya's eyes burned into the man.

It wasn't looking good.

Leo's mind raced. He glanced at Borya's gun on the concrete.

Could he get there before the man noticed?

Olezka's gun was aimed squarely at Borya's chest.

Why was he even thinking about it?

Leo had no idea how to use a gun. He didn't even know how to hold it properly. Trying to get this one, right now, would be suicide.

Borya stood in silence, breathing hard through the pain. The full power of his cold, hard glare aimed at Olezka.

"Enough talking," Olezka said. "I have a business to run. Fortunately, I have no shortage of good men to help me. Losing one is no problem. Just another bad apple." He spun to face Minty. "You have my money."

Minty didn't move.

Leo suspected, just like his, that Minty's mind was racing through options and solutions.

"Pass me the bag," Olezka said. "Now."

Minty's fingers clenched around the bag's strap.

"I need this money," Minty said, no louder than a whisper.

Olezka looked at him. A smiled parted his rubbery lips. He moved the single eye of the silenced pistol towards Minty's chest. Minty didn't move. He didn't even blink. Olezka swapped the gun to his left hand and took a step towards Minty. The gun didn't falter at all during the movement. Olezka extended his right hand to take the bag.

Everything was moving in slow motion now.

Minty took a step backwards.

"Don't make this more difficult than it needs to be," Olezka said, in a tone that suggested the pair were sharing a joke. "You give me the money, and we have no problem. My problem is with him." He indicated Borya. "As far as I care, you can go."

"I need this," Minty whispered, taking another step backwards.

"I'm sure you do," Olezka said. The thick fingers on his right hand clenched into a fist. The heavy fist swung and crunched hard into Minty's jaw.

Minty's hand shot to his face and the bag dropped.

"Thank you," Olezka said, seizing the bag and taking a step backwards. "That was the right thing to do. You wanted out, and maybe you will still get out, too. After all, I respect you. You made me lots of money. I haven't shot you yet, so maybe you will get through this. What you say..." Olezka said something in Russian and the man holding the light laughed. Borya's stare intensified.

"Hey, you know, we could keep working together, what you say?" Olezka continued talking.

Minty's shoulders slumped with dejection.

"Maybe I'll make you stay and work for me. Maybe money is not worth enough to you. No one is irreplaceable. You have already made yourself look dead, so is no problem for me to do the job properly."

71

The spy station's domes hovered against the pale wash of the sky. Behind them, the strobing lights of a plane slid across the sky. A few hours ago, that had been Allissa, arriving in the city for the first time. And now she was here, on the trail of a killer.

Voices carried on the still night air from somewhere in the tower. Allissa switched off her light and looked up at the floors of crumbling concrete. A dim glow resonated from somewhere near the top. It was a long way off, but something was up there. Someone. As Allissa watched, a beam of light swept from left to right. There was movement near the building's edge. Was that Leo?

She needed to get up there, now.

Allissa rushed past a dilapidated digger and three stacked oil cans. The entrance to the tower was just a dark hole in the concrete. Inside, the building was silent. The structure absorbed any of the shouts she'd heard outside. That meant they wouldn't see her light either. Allissa flicked on the light from her phone and ran for the stairs.

Water dripped in a constant rhythmic beat.

Berlin

Allissa took the stairs two at a time. The noise of her feet rattled from bare walls. Reaching the first floor, she looked around. The stairwell opened into a room which spanned the entire level. Treetops swayed around the tower, showing Allissa how high she had climbed. She kept going. From the ground, it looked as though the light had come from one of the top floors. After the fifth set of stairs, she paused. It couldn't be far now. She listened for any noise above the sound of her heavy breathing. Nearby, something rumbled and snapped.

Allissa covered the light with her hand and looked upwards. She was close now. For a few seconds she let her breathing subside.

Being out of breath after five flights of stairs wasn't good enough. When they got back to Brighton, she would have to start exercising more frequently. Maybe she would go running with Leo. With that thought, Allissa realised that it always seemed to come back to Leo. Any problem, any solution, any thought... it all came back to him. He was her sounding board and confidant. Her business partner, friend and —

A distant shout echoed down the stairwell. Allissa pushed on. She covered the phone's torch so that only a tiny crack of light came through her fingers, and headed for the next set of stairs.

72

Leo fought a wave of panic. They had to be okay. Something would happen, and in a few minutes they'd be walking down those stairs again.

Breathe in, breathe out. Something will happen. It'll work out.

Leo needed to stay focused. He couldn't let the panic consume him now.

"You two," the man with the gun said to Leo and Minty, "go and stand over there." He signalled for them to move backwards.

Leo focused on his breathing. He couldn't fall into a panic now.

Breathe in, breathe out. Calm, focus, breathe.

Leo and Minty took a step backwards.

He needed to stay in control now. There was no time for panic. If he didn't do what this guy asked, then he might be the one getting shot.

Leo and Minty took another step backwards. Glancing sideways at the designer, Leo noticed how ashen the man looked. It was as though he had lost more than money.

Borya and the man with the gun were exchanging words that Leo didn't understand.

Leo's mind roamed. What would happen if he died here tonight?

He thought about his sister and nephew. He should have seen them more often. He should have been there for them. Now he might not be able to help his sister with anything. Dead was no good to anyone. Leo hoped, prayed, that Andy — his sister's husband — would treat them well. If Andy could turn things around just enough to be a decent father, not even a brilliant father — just an acceptable one — then things would be okay.

Leo snatched his eyes open. The dark night. The muzzle of the gun shaking over muted words. No, he was still here.

Then, Leo thought of Mya. The woman he'd lost. The reason he'd gone to Kathmandu. The reason he'd met Allissa.

Allissa.

Mya dissolved into the darkness of Leo's thoughts and Allissa appeared like a sunrise. Leo thought of the adventures they'd shared, how they'd found each other in Kathmandu and survived the evil plans of Allissa's father. Then he thought of her in the clinging black dress. Leo felt his expression warm. Allissa made him happy and in the memory — the clinging black dress showing the curvature of her figure — she looked happy too.

Leo let the breath go. It slipped easily from his lungs.

He pulled in another one. It slid deep. Painlessly. Leo felt it nourishing every sense, cell and sinew.

Breathe in, breathe out. Calm, focus, breathe.

He repeated the mantra to himself.

"Take another step backwards." The man with the gun

was shouting at Leo and Minty. Whatever Borya had said had wound him up.

"It's time for me" — he swung his gaze, and the barrel of the gun, back towards Borya — "to take out the trash."

Then, without warning, the scene was plunged into darkness as the man holding the light crumpled to the floor.

73

"And remember" — Allissa heard the voice as she reached the bottom of the staircase — "you have already made yourself look dead, so it is no problem for me to do the job properly."

She killed the light and felt her way up the final stairs. Reaching the top, she looked out from the darkness of the stairwell. A man stood with his back to her. He was holding the torch which illuminated the scene. Another man stood further ahead. He held a gun.

Allissa took two more steps and the rest of the scene came into view. Another guy stood in the centre; his long green coat flailed in the wind.

Then she saw a fourth man. She recognised him instantly — that was Minty Rolleston. Taking another step forward, she saw Leo. He was standing next to Minty, his posture tense, his eyes flicking between the men.

Allissa stepped forward again. The man with the torch was just three feet ahead. He was laughing to himself. Clearly, he was enjoying the evening's events. Allissa sized him up from his silhouette. Although he was only six inches taller than Allissa, he must have been twice her weight. If he realised she was there, Allissa knew she'd be powerless. She needed to get this right.

Allissa raised the tyre iron above her head and focused on the man's short-cropped hair. She inhaled a deep breath and steadied herself.

"It's time for me..." said the man with the gun.

Allissa moved forwards and planted her feet securely on the concrete. If she missed or didn't get this right... she couldn't even consider it. Allissa raised the tyre iron further.

"... to take out the trash."

Three... two... one...

The tyre iron jarred against the man's skull. The man let out a short, throaty cry and slumped to the floor. The torch clattered down and went out. The scene was plunged into darkness.

The strike had found its mark.

The man was out.

Allissa leapt for the cover of the wall on the left. She expected the other man to fire when the light went out. She wasn't wrong. Three shots hissed passed and slammed into the concrete behind her. Allissa winced as she hit the floor. Two more shots exploded in the darkness. This time louder. An ear-splitting thunk reverberated through the building. Allissa's ears whined.

Another shot. Louder again. Then another.

Each one ricocheted around the building.

Allissa lay there, waiting. With each shot, she expected the crippling pain of a bullet wound. None came.

Then a light snapped on.

Glancing down at herself, Allissa didn't see any injuries.

She turned towards the light. In front of her, she saw Minty holding a gun and, on the floor, the large man lying motionless.

74

Minty wasted no time after the scene was plunged into darkness. Surging forward, he grabbed the gun and levelled it towards the source of Olezka's voice. His finger slid over the trigger and squeezed. The shot echoed around the building. Minty felt the ache of the recoil in his elbows.

He redirected the gun and fired again, and again. Finally, the chamber clicked empty.

A light came on and Minty looked around. Three pairs of eyes stared at him in shock. On the floor, already seeping with blood, lay Olezka.

Minty dropped the gun. It rattled to the floor.

Leo got to his feet and steadied Minty.

"Good work," Borya said, grabbing the gun from the floor and tucking it back beneath his coat.

Borya pulled the bag from Olezka's hand and passed it to Minty. Then he went through the man's jacket and removed a set of keys.

Allissa climbed to her feet and exhaled slowly. She stared with wide eyes at the scene until Leo caught her gaze.

"Whoever you people are," Borya said two minutes later as Leo and Allissa helped him down the stairs, "I thank you. If you hadn't been there, this would have turned out quite differently."

Minty walked behind them, carrying the bag in one hand and the torch in the other. Leo saw the early signs of shock in his vacant expression.

"We just going to leave those guys here?" Minty said, casting a glance over his shoulder.

Leo knew the memory of what Minty had done would live with him forever. But without it, Leo had no doubt they would all be dead.

"I'll get someone out here to sort it," Borya replied. "I'll call from the car. By sunrise, it'll all be sorted."

"But I... I..."

"Don't worry, Borya will sort it all. I have the gun. That'll be cleaned. They'll be no trace of you on it at all. You'll be long gone anyway." Borya looked at Allissa, who supported his left shoulder. "That guy you dealt with will no doubt come round soon and tell the rest of his *ublyudok* not to mess with me. Good work."

Borya winced as they took the final few steps.

"You need to get to a hospital," Allissa said. "You've lost a lot of blood."

"This little scratch." Borya smiled. "It'll be fine. I'll get my driver to take us past a doctor I know. Bullet wounds raise questions in hospitals."

"She's dead," Allissa said, her voice cold.

"Ah shit," Borya said, limping on. At the bottom of the stairs, he signalled for them to stop. "Take me to the car," he said, slumping against a wall. "I'll make a call, and someone will be here soon. I've got people. Don't worry."

"You'll pass out soon." Allissa looked at his blood-soaked trousers.

"Na, I'm fine, this is nothing."

Allissa took Borya's left arm and Leo grabbed his right. Together they limped across the yard. Behind them, the tower loomed into the sky. One more dark secret had now added to its nefarious history.

"She's made a real mess," Borya said, looking at the splatters of blood covering the inside of the Maserati. "No matter. I've just inherited this one." Borya removed a set of keys. The Rolls Royce clicked open. "Just put me against the front there," Borya said, pointing to the Rolls' large fender.

Allissa and Leo did as the Russian asked.

"You need to get help immediately," Leo reminded him.

"Yes, I will make a call in a moment. My contacts are only two minutes away. Would you mind," Borya said to Allissa, "getting my pipe for me, it's on the back seat of the Maserati, I think."

Allissa rolled her eyes. The guy was minutes from losing consciousness and all he was worried about was smoking a pipe. Looking at his expression though — those blue-grey eyes — Allissa wasn't going to argue.

"Thank you so much," Borya said, pulling a pouch of tobacco from his coat. "You guys should go." He pointed at Minty, who was staring into the woodland. "Look after this one."

Leo and Allissa nodded.

"I owe you my life," Borya said, as he began stuffing the pipe with tobacco. "Next time you come to Berlin, you are staying with Borya. The best time of your lives. Just ask for Borya. People know who I am."

Leo nodded, although he had no intention of finding out what Borya claimed was the best time of your life.

"And Minty," Borya said, lighting a match. The designer turned. "If you ever want to come back, you know where I am."

Without a reply, Minty began walking down the hill. Allissa and Leo followed.

After a few metres, Leo glanced back. Borya leaned against the fender of the Rolls Royce and pulled a long breath on his pipe. Removing it from his lips, he exhaled a thick cloud of white smoke. Watching the man, Leo got the impression that, whether he liked it or not, he would see the Russian again.

75

Minty switched on his torch and led Leo and Allissa into the woodland. As the darkness encroached further, Leo pulled out his torch too. The twin beams danced through the trees as the three made progress down the incline.

For a couple of minutes, no one spoke. Minty just gazed forward, his eyes unfocused, his mind no doubt re-playing the moment he had shot Olezka. Leo knew what Minty was feeling. Although Minty had saved their lives, the memory of killing someone would always live with him. It would loop constantly through his thoughts.

Leo looked at Allissa and realised how lucky it was she'd found them when she did.

At the bottom of the hill, the path widened and Leo walked alongside the others.

"Thank you," Minty said. "I suppose you'll go and tell everyone what's happened now."

"No," Allissa said, "we don't do this to make headlines. We came here to find you. We needed to check that you were alive and safe. We'll tell your family that. The rest is up to you."

Minty turned to face the pair. His eyes glistened in the torchlight.

"I wanted to tell them; I just couldn't risk it. Couldn't even risk the phone call." Minty's stare became unfocused. "If they" — he indicated behind them with a thumb — "caught up with me, there was no telling what they'd do. I wouldn't be here —"

"Whatever you were involved in," Leo said, "it's over now. You're safe."

The three walked in silence for a minute. The trees had become less dense and beyond them, the lights of suburbia glimmered. They were getting back to civilisation.

"What problem did those guys have with you?" Allissa asked.

Leo wondered the same. There were still unanswered questions about the nature of Minty's dealing with the Russians.

Minty swung his torch left and right, as though checking they were alone. When he was satisfied, he began.

"When I arrived in Berlin with the idea for the sustainable fashion retailer, I was massively ahead of my time. That sort of thing is pretty common now, but not five years ago. Stupidly, I went for it anyway. I wish now that I'd waited. I sank all the money I could into the shop, setting up the website, sourcing the best ethical materials — all that. But after about a year, things were going really badly. I just wasn't making the sales I needed. The bills were mounting up, the rent had increased, the clothes were costing more to produce than I thought. I was going to have to pack it in. I'd have lost it all… Then I got a visit from Olezka —"

"That man?" Leo signalled behind them.

Minty nodded. "He said he could help me. He seemed to know a lot about the business. He knew that my clothes were made and imported from Peru. He knew how often I got deliveries, and he knew I needed the help. He made me a deal. All I had to do was receive some other deliveries for the business. I just had to accept them and leave them in the shop for a few weeks. Then they would be collected. He said he would pay me a thousand euros per package. I didn't even need to touch or open them. Just accept them and wait. I knew it was something bad, but I didn't see how I could get blamed for it. I needed the money..."

Leo nodded and dropped behind Minty as they passed a fallen tree. Minty's voice carried through the still night air.

"That went on for years. The number of boxes increased, as did the money. For a while, it was great. I used some of the money to invest in the business and enjoyed the lifestyle. But then it all changed. The men demanded more. They started meeting in the shop, smoking in there, doing deals, taking drugs. I couldn't run a business that way. So, I told them I wanted out. I thought the business had grown a bit and that I would be alright on my own."

Minty rubbed a hand across his face. Leo wondered whether he had ever told this story before.

"Olezka, the guy I..." — Minty pointed behind them — "... he was the leader. He said no. He said I owed them. They'd done all this and that for me, and I owed them..."

Minty sniffed then rubbed the back of his right hand with his left. His shoulders slumped.

"I was so scared. I was just so scared. I... I just needed out."

The houses and streetlights were now clearly visible through the trees.

"Then Borya came to me with a proposal. For a few

weeks, we would hide some of the deliveries. We had the perfect place. It was easy because most of the time the packages were left untouched for weeks, and more arrived every day. Sometimes more than once a day. They couldn't have been keeping track. When we had enough, Borya said he knew someone who could fake a death report for me. Get me out for good. I'd then go into hiding, he'd sell all the stock we'd collected, and then we'd split the money. It was everything I needed. A fresh start. Someone must have found out, though."

"You got the money." Leo indicated the bag which swung from Minty's hand. "What are you going to do now?"

Minty looked at Leo. "We're getting out of here tonight. We've got it all planned. I've just been waiting for this." Minty nodded at the bag. "This will get us started, give us long enough to get somewhere safe. Then we'll see what happens."

A wide, suburban street materialized from the darkness of the woodland. The large houses sat in darkness.

"Will you do something for me?" Minty asked, stopping and turning to face Leo and Allissa. "I mean, I know you've done so much already... if you weren't there tonight —"

"Whatever it is, we'll try," Allissa said.

"Let *me* tell my family. I'll call them as soon as we're away from here and safe."

Leo thought of the distraught young man who had met them in their distant Brighton flat two days ago. He knew they should pass on the information straight away. But, then again, what difference did a few hours make?

"We'll wait twenty-four hours," Allissa said, speaking before Leo had decided. "This time tomorrow we'll call your brother."

Minty exhaled.

"But," Allissa said, "it would be better if we didn't have to do that at all."

"What do you —"

"It would be better If you told them yourself. You could call them on your way out of the city. You don't even have to tell them where you're going, just that you're okay. That's all they'll want to know."

Minty smiled weakly.

"This is me," Minty said, signalling towards a large house.

"You're staying here?" Leo said.

Minty nodded.

"Not exactly hiding out, is it?"

"No," Minty said, "It's not mine, though. I can't wait to leave the place, to be honest. The car's been packed and ready to go for days now. I've been freaking out at everything that's happened."

Leo knew the feeling.

"Good luck," Allissa said, extending a hand. Minty shook it.

"I'm glad we found you," Leo said.

"Thank you, again," Minty said. "I'll contact my family as soon as we're safe." He turned and begun to cross the road before pausing and looking back at Leo and Allissa. "See you around," he said, raising a hand.

"I hope not," Allissa said.

76

"There's just one thing I don't get..." Allissa said as they began to walk away. Neither she nor Leo had thought about the events of the last hour. Both still felt dazed and confused.

"I get why the guys were after him now," Allissa said. "I even understand why Minty faked his death. But why now? What changed to bring this on?" Allissa stopped and turned. "Wait a minute."

"What now? We're done. Let's get back to the hotel and —"

"No, we don't know it all. Quick, follow me." Allissa turned and walked back towards Minty's house and ducked behind the front hedge of the house opposite.

"Are you serious?" Leo followed her, grumbling.

"I just want to see," Allissa whispered. "There's something that doesn't make sense here."

"What's that?" Leo crouched beside Allissa and peered through the leaves. "Minty just wanted out, and the gangsters said no. It's pretty simple from where I'm looking."

"No, it's not. There's more to it," Allissa whispered. "He

said 'we're getting out of here tonight.' Not, *I'm* getting out of here tonight.' There's someone else involved."

Allissa glanced at Leo. Patchy shadows from the surrounding trees patterned across his face.

"Look, watch."

A light snapped on inside the house. A shadow moved through the room.

"Minty admitted that business wasn't going well," Allissa said. "Yes, he was involved in underhand dealings with the packages, but he said there was no danger. He could deny all knowledge if he wanted."

The shadow in the house disappeared for a few seconds, then another light began to blaze on the first floor. Two more quickly followed.

For five minutes Leo and Allissa watched for movement. Leo shifted his weight from one foot to the other. Then the lights of a car appeared in the driveway. The still night was disturbed by the sound of its whining engine. A VW Golf pulled out onto the road and stopped outside the front door.

Minty got out and ran to the door. He pulled the door open and a rectangle of light flooded into the street. Two suitcases sat on the hallway floor.

Leo and Allissa watched from behind the hedge as Minty carried the first suitcase to the car. He opened the rear door, slid it in and then returned for the second. As Minty forced the second suitcase into the already packed car, a dark figure walked into the door's rectangle of light.

"I told you," Allissa whispered. "*We're* getting out tonight."

Minty began to smile. It was a smile Allissa recognised. The sort of smile a person saves not just for happiness, but for someone they love. Giving the suitcase a final shove,

Berlin

Minty slammed the car door and scampered towards the silhouette.

All Allissa could see was a dark shape against the light. A woman, she assumed by the long hair and body shape. Minty whispered something to the woman and kissed her cheek. Then, taking the woman's arm, Minty led her down the stairs. Watching from behind the bush, it suddenly made sense to Allissa. She understood why Minty needed out. Why he needed to leave his life with the Russian gangsters and mysterious packages. Why he would risk anything to get away. And why he even felt the pain caused to his family was justifiable.

The woman, who took the steps slowly with Minty's assistance, was heavily pregnant.

77

It all made sense, as Minty opened the car's front passenger door and helped the woman clamber in. Minty needed a new life. He needed to start again. He needed to do it properly because he was going to become a dad.

"I told you," Allissa whispered, beaming in the darkness.

Leo nodded. Allissa was right. The risks involved with mysterious packages from the Russians may have been acceptable for a man on his own, but Minty would have felt differently faced with the prospect of being a father. Children changed things.

"People don't change for no reason," Allissa said.

Minty climbed up to the house for the last time.

"No," Leo agreed. "You're right."

"Circumstances change people," Allissa said. "Sometimes for the bad, but sometimes for good."

As Minty locked the house, Leo found himself grinning. He glanced at Allissa beside him and felt a flourishing warmth.

Minty posted the keys through the letterbox, then

turned. He looked right and left, up and down the street. The habit of someone used to checking over their shoulder perhaps, or someone saying goodbye to a place that had protected him and his family.

Minty wrapped a bright yellow scarf around his shoulders and, with a broad smile, looked directly at Leo and Allissa. Leo stumbled further out of sight. With his smile unfaltering, Minty waved.

"Bugger," Leo whispered.

Minty turned to a large plant pot next to the door and removed a camera from amongst the leaves. He had been watching the street the whole time.

"Clever guy," Allissa said as they stood up.

Minty looped the scarf around his shoulders and got in the car. For a moment, the engine's gentle purring was the only sound, then the car clunked into gear and pulled away.

Leo stepped out onto the road to watch it go and raised a hand too. At the end of the street, the car turned left. A yellow scarf fluttered from the window.

That's west, Leo thought, *perhaps Hamburg, or Hanover. Or anywhere else.* That was the best thing. No one knew where they were going. Not even Minty.

78

"This way," Leo said, starting in the direction of the station. "What time is it?"

Allissa checked her phone. "Just before five."

"The trains should be running again by now. The station's just up here."

The pair walked in silence.

Leo's mind twisted and turned with the events of the evening.

Ahead, a pair of starlings darted across the path and landed on a branch overhanging the road. Their chirruping song pierced the silence. As Leo and Allissa approached, the birds leapt into flight again.

"One question," Leo and Allissa both said at the same time.

Realizing the coincidence, they looked at each other.

"You go," Allissa said, her expression fierce.

"No, you," Leo said, trying in vain to appear serious.

He yelped as he felt Allissa's elbow dig him in the ribs.

"What! What was that for —"

"Why didn't you keep in touch with me?" Allissa's

expression darkened. "We're supposed to be a team, which means you keep me involved."

"I know, I was tracking Borya. Couldn't exactly ring you."

"A message would have been fine. I was worried about you."

Allissa walked ahead and Leo ran three steps to catch up.

The starlings watched from their perch on the branch.

"How did you find me?" Leo asked.

"Remember the 'Find Your Phone' app?" Allissa asked, pulling out her phone.

"Ahh yeah," Leo said, tapping his pockets. "Oh shit! Borya made me give the phone to Anafisa. I've got to go back and —"

"Leave it," Allissa said, her expression thawing. "We're not going back there now. If the police aren't there already, they soon will be."

Leo looked at Allissa. Circumstances had forced him to travel across the world for her, and now she'd done the same for him. They both risked their lives for what was right, and for each other.

"I'm sorry I didn't keep in touch," Leo said.

"And…"

"And what?"

"Thank you for saving my arse, again…" Allissa said.

"Well," Leo said, "I had it totally under control. I would have —"

Allissa silenced him with a look before quickening her pace.

Leo watched her and smiled.

One starling shuffled closer to the other on the branch. Their rhythmic twitter mingled with the dawn.

Looking at Allissa, her face awash with the glow of the

coming morning, Leo thought about the embrace they'd shared a few days before. Right now, he wanted that more than anything.

Leo took a few quick steps and caught up with Allissa. Inhaling a reinforcing breath, he lifted his arm and put it around Allissa's shoulders.

"What're you doing?" Allissa said, looking up at him.

"I've just missed you, I suppose," Leo said, leaning towards her.

"Go put your arm around Borya," Allissa retorted, shrugging off Leo's arm and accelerating again.

Leo watched and laughed. Maybe one day, he thought, circumstances would let him close that final distance.

Allissa paused and looked back at Leo. Her beaming smile showed that she had missed him too.

Leo didn't notice though; he was watching the starlings skitter together in the direction of the woodland.

EPILOGUE

"So, let me get this right," Allissa said as she walked towards Leo sat at the desk in their front room. Through the window, the grey-blue patchwork of the sky looked cold. Leo had wedged the ancient sash window open with a guidebook, and fresh salty air streamed in. "She wants us to follow her husband there, just to see what he gets up to?"

"That's it." Leo spun on the chair to face her. "I know we don't usually take this sort of jealous marital stuff, but —"

Leo and Allissa got offers of work from wives and husbands all the time. Generally, the missing partner had just left because the relationship had run its course. The client didn't need the services they offered, but those of a therapist.

"What's the difference here?"

Leo spun to his computer. Allissa saw the map of an island she didn't recognised on the screen.

"She knows where he is, for one."

"So, he's not actually missing —"

"No."

"So, why are we doing it?"

"This is where he is." Leo tapped the map, and the image of a flawless beach filled the screen. Clear blue water lapped against white sand. Palm trees hung lazily. "And she's going to fly us there and book us into a five-star hotel just down the road from where her husband is."

"And what do we have to do?" Allissa wasn't convinced. It sounded too good to be true.

"We just have to monitor who comes and goes from his house. She's not even said why — just monitor. I said we weren't into trespassing and that. She said that was fine. The house has a long approach road we could sit out of sight on."

"Oh, so we've got to sit in a mosquito-infested bush all day in some tropical paradise."

"Well, we would." Leo clicked to another internet browser. "If I hadn't just ordered this."

Allissa leaned in to see the screen. It was a battery-operated remote-control camera system attached to a stake that could be pushed into any flower bed, bush or pot plant.

"Didn't we see —" Allissa said.

"Yep, Minty had one outside his house. That's how the sneaky bugger saw we were spying on him. It just got me thinking how useful something like that could be, and then this lady contacted us —"

"Is it legal?"

"I... I don't know." Leo spun back to the computer screen. "It doesn't say. But do you really care? We'll put this thing near the guy's house, and we can watch the lot from beside the pool."

"I see." Allissa straightened up, beaming. "Now we're talking. When do we leave?"

Leo's answer was disturbed by the buzz of the flat's door entry system.

"Oh, that thing's working." Allissa turned towards the door where the handset and screen were mounted on the wall. Allissa picked up the phone and looked at the screen. Black and white lines flickered, but no picture materialised. A distorted, incomprehensible voice cracked from the speaker.

"I'll come down," she said into the handset before replacing it on the cradle. "Nope, still knackered."

With their company being registered to the flat, they got multiple deliveries every day. The problem was, the intercom didn't work, so delivery drivers often assumed no one was in and took the parcel to the sorting office, which was nearly two miles away.

Allissa rushed down the three twisting flights of stairs. She really didn't want to have to go there again. Turning onto the final staircase, Allissa saw a dark outline through the glass door.

Good, he's still there.

Stepping over multiple piles of junk mail and moving the bike, which always seemed to be in the way, Allissa opened the door.

"Hi," she said, out of breath. She would get into an exercise routine soon. "Sorry it took so long. The system's broken and we're on the top floor."

"Parcel for Leo Keane," the rider said, his voice muffled by his motorcycle helmet. The visor of his helmet was raised; Allissa felt his pale blue-grey eyes connect with hers. There was something about those eyes that said, *I get what I want.*

"Yeah, sure, I'll take that." Allissa reached out and took the package. It was no bigger than a paperback book.

"Thanks, have a great day," the rider said, turning. Allissa recognised an accent. Eastern European, or even Russian.

"Thanks," she shouted as the man turned and walked towards his bike. He had a pronounced limp on his left leg.

Allissa pushed the door shut and climbed the stairs again.

"I've e-mailed to say we'll do it," Leo shouted as Allissa let the door slam behind her. "She's going to send the deposit for the flights and hotel today. It could be a nice little earner."

"Cool." Allissa crossed the room and placed the package on his desk. "We best get packing."

"What's this?" Leo picked it up.

"No idea, probably some shit you've ordered online that we've no use for."

Leo turned it over in his hands. "I don't remember ordering anything." Leo pulled the strip seal from the packet and looked inside. "What the...?" he muttered as a mobile phone fell into his hand.

Leo looked at Allissa.

The phone felt familiar. Leo pressed the screen, and the phone recognised his finger. A picture filled the screen. It was a picture Leo had taken of the hills surrounding Pokhara. He'd had the image as his phone background for ages. It was the phone Leo had last seen in the back of the red Maserati.

New York

In their next case, Leo and Allissa go to one of the most written about cities on the globe — New York.

Berlin

I visited New York for the first time in 2018 and, as with all my settings, just longed to write a story there.

Read New York now:
www.lukerichardsonauthor.com/newyork

"Luke Richardson has pulled this one out of the bag."

"I love this series. New York is my favourite."

"A superb thriller"

"I love the work of this author and recommend all of his books."

A SERIAL KILLER stalks the streets. The city lives in fear. **The winter of terror is here.**

Heading to New York for a much-needed holiday, Andy and Emma hope some quality time will put their relationship back on track. But, when Andy wrecks his car in the Lincoln Tunnel and then disappears, it's clear the city that never sleeps has other plans.

Teaming up with New York P.I. Niki Zadid, Leo and Allissa search the city. But this isn't just another case, Emma's Leo's sister, he knew they were having problems, and should've done more to help.

When their investigation entangles with the plans of an unhinged killer, things become more complex and dangerous than any had imagined. The trio must navigate the city, from elite hangouts to dingy back streets, without falling foul of a murderer with a sickening endgame in mind.

New York is Luke Richardson's fifth fiery international thriller. Grab your copy to continue this series today!

www.lukerichardsonauthor.com/newyork

WHAT HAPPENED IN KOH TAO?

Read the series prequel novella for free now:
www.lukerichardsonauthor.com/kohtao

"Intense, thrilling, mysterious and captivating."

"The story grabs you, you're on the boat with your stomach pitching. As the story gathers pace the tension is palpable. It's a page turner which keeps you hooked until the final word."

 "

The evocative writing takes you to a place of white sand, the turquoise sea and tranquilly. But on an island of injustice and exploitation, tranquillity is the last thing Leo finds."

"Love and adventure collide in Thailand, love it!"

KOH TAO

Leo's looking for the perfect place to propose to the love of his life. When they arrive in the Thai tropical paradise of Koh Tao, he thinks he's found it.

But before he gets an answer, she's nowhere to be seen.

On searching the resort, his tranquillity turns to turmoil. Is it a practical joke? Has she run away? Or is it something much more sinister?

Set two years before Luke Richardson's international thriller series, this compulsive novella turns back the clock on an anxiety ridden man battling powerful forces in a foreign land.

KOH TAO is the prequel novella to Luke Richardson's international thriller series. Grab your copy for free and find out where it all began!

www.lukerichardsonauthor.com/kohtao

Music has been a big part of my life for a long as I can remember and this is the first one of my novels to include it. I loved writing Leo's visit to the nightclub. The DJs mentioned are friends of mine too – although they may be so underground that even Google doesn't know about them (yet). As such, I dedicate this book to everyone I've danced with. Whist there are way too many of you to mention by name, and I am bound to offend by trying, know that the moments we've spent getting lost in the music are very special to me.

I do want to make a special mention, though, to those who are now dancing, singing and partying elsewhere:

Peter Clough
Craig "Chopper" Hutchinson
and Paul Revill
To quote the 1998 hit by house music trio Stardust, "the music sounds better with you."

JOIN MY MAILING LIST

During the years it took me to write plan and this book, I always looked to its publication as being the end of the process. The book would be out, and the story would be finished.

Since releasing it in May 2019, I realised that putting the book into the world was actually just the start. Now I go on the adventure with every conversation I have about it. It's so good to hear people's frustrations with Leo's reserve, their shock at the truth about the grizzly backstreet restaurant, and their questions about what's going to happen next.

Most of these conversations happen with people on my mailing list, and I'd love you to join too.

I send an email a couple of times a month in which I talk about my new releases, my inspirations and my travels.

Sign up now:

www.lukerichardsonauthor.com/mailinglist

OTHER BOOKS BY LUKE RICHARDSON

Leo & Allissa International Thrillers

Koh Tao
www.lukerichardsonauthor.com/kohtao

Kathmandu
www.lukerichardsonauthor.com/kathmandu

Hong Kong
www.lukerichardsonauthor.com/hongkong

Berlin
www.lukerichardsonauthor.com/berlin

New York
www.lukerichardsonauthor.com/newyork

Riga
www.lukerichardsonauthor.com/riga

The Liberator: Kayla Stone Vigilante Thrillers

Justice is her beat

Her name is Kayla Stone

She is 'The Liberator'

The Liberator Series is a ferocious new collaboration between Luke Richardson and Amazon Bestseller, Steven Moore.

If you like Clive Cussler, Nick Thacker, Ernest Dempsey and Rusesel Blake, then you'll love this explosive new series!

www.lukerichardsonauthor.com/theliberator

THANK YOU

Thank you for reading *Berlin*. Sharing my writing with you has been a dream of many years. Thank you for making it a reality.

As may come across in my writing, travelling, exploring and seeing the world is so important to me, as is coming home to my family and friends.

Although the words here are my own, the characters, experiences and some of the events described are wholly inspired by the people I've travelled beside. If we shared noodles from a street-food vendor, visited a temple together, played cards on a creaking overnight train, or had a beer in a back-street restaurant, you are forever in this book.

It's the intention of my writing to show that although the world is big and the unknown can be unsettling, there is so much good in it. Although some of the people in my stories are bad and evil – the story wouldn't be very interesting if they weren't – they're vastly outnumbered by the honesty, purity and kindness of the other characters. You don't have to look far to see this in the real world. I know that whenever I travel, it's the kindness of the people that I remember

Thank you

almost more than the place itself. Whether you're an experienced traveller, or you prefer your home turf, it's my hope that this story has taken you somewhere new and exciting.

Again, thank you for coming on the adventure with me, I hope to see you again.

Luke

PS. A little warning, next time someone talks to you in the airport, be careful what you say, as you may end up in their book.

BOOK REVIEWS

If you've enjoyed this book I would appreciate a review.

Reviews are essential for three reasons. Firstly, they encourage people to take a chance on an author they've never heard of. Secondly, bookselling websites use them to decide what books to recommend through their search engine. And third, I love to hear what you think!

Having good reviews really can make a massive difference to new authors like me.

It'll take you no longer than two minutes, and will mean the world to me.

www.lukerichardsonauthor.com/reviews

Thank you.

Printed in Great Britain
by Amazon

74852442R00154